THE
RUCTION

Book 1 in the Renascence Series

James W Powell

Published by
Wandering Stream
Literary and Publishing
Richland, WA

Interior illustrations by Donna Rey

Cover design and book publication by

Wandering Stream
Literary and Publishing

Dedicated to
my Dad
Arthur E Powell
1924-1957

I think you would have been
pleasantly surprised.

The Ruction   d

Table of Contents

Who summons archer, angel and mighty warrior?
Who beckons buck and doe for humble service?
Who carves roadways in ancient melt
And broad paths through young forest?
Who creates havens in shaded underwood
A hidden sweetness for the parched
And sustenance from naught?

Forget the former times and your age-old story
What I do is fresh and new
You'll wonder its form; muse its truth
Ponder its tool and taste its fruit
Yet it remains

Wild florae intones its praise
Feral faunae croon their creator
Seers improvise unseen clefs
And score staffs for blessing
My symphonies play odes for hope
My ruction rends the chains of hell
And fills highways of life with traffic to freedom

PROLOGUE

Grindlay, a village outside of a small town at the base of the most beautiful mountains in the country. Blessed with sufficient rainfall, its landscape is fresh and green until early summer. Different wildflowers bloom from month to month, painting colors on a grand scale.

The sounds of Grindlay Village by day are the running creek waters, birds chirping, roosters crowing and dogs barking. Bleating from kid goats searching for a meal and doe goats responding to their young ring through the neighborhood.

By night, owls hoot and the ring-tail cats shriek their cry to scare rodents from hiding. The night sky is filled with the clouds of a billion suns and the reflected shine of distant planets. Cool breezes sweep down the mountains to refresh the land. It's rustic, it's quaint and peaceful.

Roee grew up in an agricultural community where life was safe and the average person risked little to advance their social station generation after generation. Families worked hard to build and pass on their possessions and core values without giving thought that something greater could be built with inspiration, imagination and the understanding that there truly is something else to build.

Yes, over time houses became bigger and retirements more comfortable. But as it often goes, the greater treasures are lost in the pursuit of the smaller ones. The truth is, smaller seem important because they shine brighter and capture our hearts because we are told from our entry into this world that they are the essence of life.

Peculiar isn't it? We buy into shiny brilliance and capital empires as the markers of our identity. Yet, the greatest treasure of all is a humble ordinary life filled to the brim with invisible goodness.

Roee tried finding an identity in success and social status only to fail. In each instance he lost it all through circumstances beyond his control. Wealth and security were fickle friends who deserted him when he put his trust in them. Through the losses he saw something better.

Because of these trials, he found an internal freedom from needing these things and discovered instead the peace of a country existence. Retreating to Grindlay Village, he and his wife Dodee, simplified things and joined with a community of like-minded neighbors who helped each other make a better life.

Now, they raise their own food, share the benefits of community garden planning, collective ideas, ancient herbal remedies, lots of fresh air and an active faith. It's ordinary in a yesteryear sort of way.

But there was one thing waiting outside the box of their anticipation.....the God factor.

Ordinary people, that's Roee and Dodee. And that

could be anybody.

A thought, a wild idea, a passing picture in the mind; things of potential that go by as flotsam on the currents of life's river. When acted on, these ignored inspirations may be the next social breakthrough that changes the world, the next entrepreneurial blockbuster, the next creative idea for a movie or book; ordinary stuff that gets passed off as insignificant. But oh, how ordinary can morph to extraordinary when a seed thought gets planted in the contemplative mind of a creative person.

Do ordinary people wake up with an expectation that a today experience will propel them into another realm? It isn't practical to remain dialed into such a heightened level of readiness. Yet, in a single moment, a slight gust in the wind of change alters the course of destiny.

From early childhood good fathers have trained their children to anticipate the future. To anticipate the questions we are going to be asked so we can have well thought out answers. To prepare for a comfortable life in old age and leave an inheritance for their children. To foresee how to provide for themselves and others we love if something awful should happen.

God beckons us to put our lives in his hands. And oh how that irritates a soul who possesses the propensity for self determination and sufficiency. Many people are convinced God can't be trusted because he enjoys ship-wrecking our plans. It's worth considering the idea that God has good plans for us. And he loves to reveal his creative ideas to those who are listening. God, the endlessly creative person, can change any condition on the planet with a seedling of an idea. He seeks someone willing to act on it.

While some plot, plan, determine and calculate, there are those who see an invisible realm filled with life, love, adventures and dreams. Seers by faith, they know it's there. Through experience, they learn to grasp its reality.

Once that bridge is crossed, everything changes. This world loses its inherent value. Visible things become the distraction; the invisible our destination.

How do we get there?

It's simple. Become ordinary. But be prepared to change your normals.

The stories of old opened with "once upon a time." It's been setting up plots for a very long time. The expectation of that phrase provokes the hope of a happy ending.

But this story starts "One ordinary day...."

That's when the ruction occurs.

"So, what's the ruction?" you may ask.

It's a ruckus with an attitude; a riotous disturbance. It's the defining moment that turns an ordinary person toward somewhere and something they had never dreamed.

THE SHEPHERD

The morning's twilight reminds us that parts of life are constantly predictable. The sun will rise and set. What happens in between those events may be filled with hope that portentous events will not occur; dreams and intentions will find their objectives.

Both events are appreciated by dreamers and achievers alike. When noticed at all, they remind us to balance what we are doing with what we are becoming and our beginning toward or against our end.

With Roee, sunsets reflect his world. From sunrise, he's diligent to make a difference and create something personally meaningful. Sunsets are a time to contemplate his advances.

On two occasions, he built significant holdings with natural talents and sufficiency. His first attempt crashed with an unanticipated economic downturn. After a season of disappointment, he reenergized momentum and a significant rally toward what he thought could be success.

His second journey changed when he met Dodee. Falling in love with her redefined his values and priorities. And needing to know how to love redefined his relationship with his redeemer. The process birthed a determination to pursue different goals in life.

Roee loves the mountains and country living. As a child, he was drawn to the natural wonder of this part of creation. When his parents took him to the mountains, he felt a oneness with the outdoors; it was home. As time to depart approached, the thought was emotionally unbearable.

Practical realities forced him to be responsible and earn a living. Yet with that understanding came hope that he could someday own a mountain property and live his dream.

Intense would not describe Dodee's love for the outdoors, but it was strong enough and she was willing from the start to commit to the lifestyle Roee was so passionate about. For him, her companionship to share his dream was like the sunrise for a new day.

As darkness blooms from shadow to light and then to brilliance, sunrises give Roee the occasion to reaffirm his dependence on the Master Potter for what is formed inside of him and gratefulness for the pleasures that surround him. It is also an enjoyable opportunity to drink of the rich presence of Papa's company.

As an owner of two goats and assorted farm critters, daily life in Grindlay Village is mostly predictable; like knowing the sun will rise and set each day. Appreciating its variations however small, is a basic value.

Even with slight clouds, sunrises fill with color as the sun winks underneath them for a moment before regaining its dominion over them. Shades of crimson, hues of gold and orange and the slivers of silvery white separating them, last long enough to stir emotions of awe and kick-start the soul.

On cloudless days, the horizon joins with shadow until the first crescent of sun peaks through the forest on the hills to the east. The tallest trees cast silhouettes in majestic praise of another day, honoring the sun's creator.

For the shepherd, those early hours spent with Papa are like the garden experiences Adam had in the beginning. He receives instruction of sonship and fatherhood and rekindles his heart to devoted service.

As it is with intimate friends, each encounter is different and yet the same. The affectionate result of their time together is predictable. Its practical display has a variety of influences.

On this day, Roee woke with a longing to be with Papa. Finding a favorite meeting place at a fallen tree that is positioned uphill and overlooking the village, he settled in to watch the skyline. A tune rose from his heart and he hummed affection into the surrounding atmosphere.

Their friendship is seasoned. Questions are not necessarily the catalyst for conversation nor are a flow of words essential language for intimate communication. For Papa and the shepherd, their two hearts coming together as one is enough.

The shepherd's humming grew livelier as love-words bubbled into song from within.

"From the rising of the sun, until its going down,

You're my King and worthy of my praise.

You join my heart like the light from dawn,

The clouds of joy from me are drawn,

Where the life from your love is raised."

"And when I come to you, you're always there,

In faithfulness you always care.

And like the sun, your presence shines,

Like jewels and gems from earthly mines.

My life reflects your grace like moon and stars"

"Who is like you Lord my King,

Who hears my heart when praise I sing

I am a prince to stand and bring

My love to your throne."

"As friends we are joined in heart.

Your love my King will never part.

When I'm overwhelmed, I cannot be taken,

Because of you, I'm never shaken.

You are my rock and firm foundation."

As the shepherd brings his hands to his heart....

"There is no one who loves like you

There is no one who lives like you

There is no one who gives like you

I love you Papa with all my heart"

Words subside and his heart continued with the tune and reflection about his Father's love. Deep peace envelopes him as he waits in a secret spiritual place known only to him and Papa.

While he is taking in the sunrise and the intimate moment with Papa, a seemingly tangible vision enveloped him. He saw one of his two she goats running off into a wilderness. In this vision, her hooves are made of gold. He shouted to her, "Maria, come back!" The vision disappeared leaving wonder in its vacuum.

Papa just spoke in a way he had only heard about. His mind had no precedent of how to respond to this new experience.

Roee cherishes the mysteries and puzzles Papa

The Shepherd

gives him. And Papa delights in the fact Roee pays careful attention to those mysteries and will search for their meanings. Experience has increased Roee's proficiency for putting together the pieces of Papa's frequent surprises.

He continued to sit quietly, pondering questions and waiting for comment;

"Papa, what do you want me to do with this?"

"Is Maria in some kind of trouble?"

"What is this about, Papa?"

"Go and pursue, my son, I will be with you."

It's the only clue Papa gave to solve this mystery.

The shepherd stepped into the cabin where he and the shepherdess had been living a few years and shut the door. He was lost in troubled thought yet mixed with assurance that Papa was involved. He was piqued by the golden hooves in the vision; its meaning significant.

Without a moment's hesitation, Dodee looked up and spoke with concern.

"Roee, Maria is missing, I can't find her anywhere. I followed her tracks to the edge of the forest and they light out from there. I can't imagine what could have spooked her, honey. It's not like her to wander away!"

"I need to go after her and bring her home, Dodee. I came back for some stuff to take with me. No telling what I'll run into out there. But, I'm confident she will be just fine." He shared with Dodee the vision he had that morning, assuring her that Maria was in good hands.

"It is to the glory of God to conceal mysteries," Dodee began with an encouraging smile, "and it is for the glory of a king to figure it out. You are a kingly and wise man, my love. Papa said he will be with you, so that settles it. I will be praying."

Roee strapped on a hand gun for protection from the predators roaming the woods, then grabbed a hatchet and a couple day's provision. His shepherd's staff in hand, he set out to find Maria and unpack the secret put before him.

With a couple of weeks until spring, he left with substantial daylight remaining.

Goats graze in meandering paths, yet cover great distances in a day if left to themselves. Roee hoped for good forage to be available wherever she was going. It should slow her down and make it easier to catch up with her.

Regardless of his hopes, he reluctantly thought it prudent to bring his hatchet for cutting firewood. It may be necessary to spend a night in the forest.

The Shepherd

The morning of his second day of tracking Maria, Roee's inner thoughts mirrored the frustration of the previous evening.

"It just isn't like Maria to wander off like that," he thought. "Goats don't go anywhere alone.....ever. Wherever one goes, they all go. The flocking instinct is such a big part of their survival and social makeup. Unless she was driven off, it's just not goat-like."

In the morning twilight, Roee spent several minutes stewing over Maria and stirring the coals of the fire he used to keep warm while he slept. The fire was cool enough to leave behind. For good measure he poured precious drinking water over the whole thing and saw no steam from the embers.

His night's rest helped to relieve last night's concern. He reminded himself that Papa is an active part of what is going on at the moment. While setting his sights on following Maria's trail, he set his heart on the one who will answer the other questions stirring in his mind: "What happened to Maria? What drove her away from her familiar surroundings? Will I find her alive?"

Before the previous day's fretting could get a foothold, he caught his thoughts and changed his speech to words of gratefulness and truth. "Thank you Papa, for always being there for me. Your way of doing things aren't anything like the way I do things. Your thoughts are so much bigger than my meager thinking. Today I make the choice to believe you will work everything out for your good purposes. I choose to trust you without reservation."

As he made his declarations, calm rose in his spirit from a secret place where Papa is given an internal home. From that peace Roee asked: "Is there anything you want to say to me this morning that I need to hear?"

The shepherd had a determination to listen for Papa's voice. From experience he knew to set aside notions about how Papa wanted to answer his questions. Responses can be words, dreams, signs in natural surroundings or visions. On a few occasions, simple answers came through weighty global events.

Papa's vocabulary is creatively large and Roee's experience includes a small list. There are ways of hearing with more than just ears; sight and smell and unusual feelings in the atmosphere.

He didn't always get it right, but Papa is a kind and patient teacher. Papa trains him for the "real thing" by practicing the "real thing" when it isn't critical and advises correction.

Roee spent the larger part of the day watching and waiting for a word from Papa while he continued his attentive pursuit of Maria. He enjoyed the natural beauty of the higher elevation. Trees and occasional meadows had been a refreshing change from the pasturage in the lower valley.

Wild berry vines produce sweet energy in the pre-spring warmth. Maria's hoof prints led him to these occasional refreshments as the hours wore on. It appeared Maria had been leading him to provision unwittingly.

Goats enjoy berry vines; thorns and all. A goat's

existence centers around eating; a primary focus shared with many creatures. It can drive them into unfamiliar places they don't need to be.

As the shepherd reflected on these things, an epiphany came and went. As he struggled to recapture the thought, he forgot about listening and watching. When he wasn't expecting it, a small quiet voice spoke, "You have been faithful, my son, to the few and small things I have given you to do. Now I will do something new with you and increase your labors for me and your reward for watching over my purposes. Be fearless. I am sending you for a peculiar and unique purpose, a fruitful mission."

Roee thought about what he heard. It dawned on him this word was an added message to the mystery. It changed the way he was viewing this journey. This was no longer about the rescue of a lost goat. It is a quest to possess a new assignment. The niggling anxiety about Maria stopped in that moment.

Before resuming his adventure the shepherd took time to sit and journal what Papa spoke to him. He wanted to share it accurately with Dodee when he returned home. As he stood from a few minutes of writing, he began to hum a melody.

Through an opening in the woods, the shepherd watched as the sun slipped into a blue envelope. Contemplative, he trudged slowly forward, watching for a good place to stop for the night. It had been a long day of uphill hiking. Despite the fact he was in good physical condition, he conceded he was not accustomed to the length of effort.

He found a potential spot, fluffed some pine needles and leaves for a cushion and threw down his bed roll.

Starting a small fire for warmth, he nestled in. Sleep came easy.

Sleeping light helps to remain aware of the nocturnal wildlife. There are critters to avoid that are looking for food. Roee knows from experience about bears and mountain lions in these woods. Perhaps more seriously, there are skunks and raccoons roaming around in families in search of groceries.

Roee loves the open air; a second home as it were. Being a learned and tested outdoorsman, he wisely put the food he brought in a bear bag; hanging it from a pair of trees with a cotton rope and away from his campfire.

But hanging his food wouldn't keep a determined raccoon from making the climb to get at it. And anyone who has encountered a skunk knows a visit from them is not amusing either.

Deep sleep while in the woods is not necessarily a good thing. Nonetheless, the shepherd couldn't help falling into a persistent slumber. He began to dream. In his dream, a messenger appeared to him standing near the campfire.

"I have come to impart to you new tools and abilities for the assignment awaiting you. You will no longer need the weapons of man, but the weapons and wisdom of the Kingdom of Heaven. Nothing can come between you and our Father's love. So do not be afraid. Be bold and courageous." The angel took a hot ember from the campfire and touched it to Roee's chest just over his heart.

Waking to warmth spreading through his entire being, the sensation of fire increased and spread like liquid to places deeper than his material body. It flowed through his mind, his soul, his mouth, ears, eyes, feet and hands. No words could explain what was going on. A change was happening to him and he had no revelation about what it was.

Because of this second occasion of being told to not be afraid, he concluded there would be opportunity to be such. When these events come, he will have to choose courage.

It took the shepherd a couple of hours before he could return to sleep. Rekindling the light of the fire, he wrote down his experience in as much detail as he could remember.

Roee was jerked awake by what he perceived to be the sound of talking. Following the voice, he determined it was coming from a tree near his bear bag. Getting up, he crept toward the voices and made his approach as not to create a defensive response from whatever may be attempting to pilfer his goods. Because the campfire had died down, his night vision was working well.

He spotted movement of an animal around the rope going over the branch where his supplies hung. There were more of these critters at the base of the tree watching for something to drop from above. What happened next could only be described as incredible.

"Those idiot humans are always trying to keep their food from us. Don't they know it belongs to us once they get out here? This is a lot of work for just a few crumbs!"

"What did you say?" yelled Rohee, surprised and unable to restrain himself.

"Ahhhhhhhhhh!" screamed all the raccoon family in response.

"Run children, run!" bellowed mama raccoon.

Furry bodies screamed and tumbled over each other at the base of the tree. They were bent on escaping the carnage they knew was certain to come upon them. Those on the ground melted quickly into the forest in fearful flight, while the one in the tree went higher exceeding the reach of the monster below. The atmosphere was thick with the weight of terror.

Reeling from the occurrence, Roee had trouble collecting his thoughts.

"Papa, what's going on here?" he thought.

Feeling the heavy weight of the raccoon family's distress he spoke quietly into the night air.

"Peace, perfect peace.....come."

A calm oozed from everywhere. It formed in the air and came out of the ground. The surrounding creation responded to the presence that enveloped the atmosphere. It was Papa's presence; in greater measure than what Roee expected. It was a moment of awe and wonder, fear and delight rolled into one. The shepherd began to chuckle because he didn't know what else to do.

He looked up at the animal in the tree and said, "Raccoon, you're free to go."

Father raccoon looked down at Roee, then to the victuals hanging from the tree and back again to the human.

"Leave the food. I'm going to need it. There's plenty for you and your family out here."

Having made his declaration, he began to laugh quietly again. Still puzzled, he considered the idea that this encounter might just be the first of many.

"Such a weird idea of carrying on conversations with animals," he thought to himself. "Storybook stuff."

While father raccoon stole away into the night, the shepherd's laughter intensified until his face and sides ached. His hilarity filled the forest and his spirit with a new kind of life.

As laughter subsided, he reflected on the picture taking shape in his thoughts. Reigniting the campfire, he wrote those thoughts while resisting the temptation to make hard and fast conclusions. He was still work-ing the clues for solving his mystery. Whatever picture he imagined at this point, was certain to be enormously incomplete.

The exhilarating stimulation of the pre-dawn morning along with the processing of this event fixed the prospect there would not be further sleep. The morning twilight was arriving.

The Visitor

When the fog in Maria's mind cleared just before sunrise, she was puzzled. The last thing she recalled was being with Carrie and grazing in the field around their home.

Had she eaten some strange thing? How long had she been wandering? What was that odd noise she heard as her mind started to clear? Where was she? There were too many questions without answers.

Behind her was a semi-dense forest, wild berry vines and patches of underbrush. Before her was a landscape of what appeared to be a very attractive and peaceful valley.

Directly in front was a delicious-looking meadowland lined at the south side with random manzanita, low growing shrubs and very old oak trees sprinkled with pines. The meadow long, wide and spacious for about one hundred yards, dog-legged to the right with a quickly sweeping turn. Oddly, there was a patch of yellow daffodils blooming at the crook of the dogleg where the other end of the meadow disappeared. About fifty feet long, the patch hugged the edge of the trees.

At the north and south sides of the valley swelled low mountains climbing a thousand feet or better above the valley floor. The north side was well forested with digger pines, cedars and occasional oak trees. Sculpted sections of rock gave the appearance of cliffs and chiseled shelves.

The steady gurgle of a creek in the distance capture Maria's attention. Reminded of her thirst and rattled about her circumstances, she strolled toward the sound and sampled eatables as she went.

Maria felt edgy being out in the open alone. It wasn't socially acceptable for a goat to be by herself; they inherently gather with family and friends.

She had heard stories about mountain lions and bears....."predators" the other animals called them. Creatures that carried away loners, never to be heard from again. Or they would kill for the sport of the hunt.

She knows the flock should always stay together no matter how frightening their situation as a safeguard. She felt lonely and vulnerable. Fighting fear, she trotted to nearby brush cover where she could hide and continue her search for water.

The hiddenness calmed her uncertainty and her jittery nerves. Her clarity of thinking increased and helped to control her fears.

"It would be great to have another girl to talk to," she wished as she thought of her sister, Carrie, back home. The two of them could talk about anything and everything, even calming the smallest storms.

Her mind's ear tuned the sound of the creek to the background while she foraged. Then a clearing under a dense tree growth revealed a haven where a drink could

The Visitor

be had safely. The odors in the air told her other animals had been there. In spite of her cautions, thirst overruled common sense. She ventured into the current until it covered her hooves and she drank deeply of the cool water.

A noise behind her triggered her reflexes. She launched forward and out of the creek without thinking. Frightened, she spun around nervously to see what had joined her. She shook her head unwillingly. Opposite her were three animals she had not seen the likes of before. The surprise of it left her wondering.

Two of them questioned her at the same time: "You're a visitor here. What are you?" while the other one said: "Where did you come from?"

Maria was tempted to run. But where could she go? She glanced around for a place to hide while thinking about what to say. The two kept asking questions, which didn't help the situation. The grilling intensified, along with her failing composure.

"What's the problem?" "Are you hurt?" "Can you talk?" "Maybe you're just dumb!"

When the third one joined the questioning, she screamed: "Sto-o-o-o-o-o-p!"

It was followed by silence. Open mouths gaped while Maria slowly crossed the stream and stood bravely in front of them.

"I'm a goat and...." she began. But before she could finish, the others broke out in wild laughter. Maria shook her head and muttered to herself: "Oh dear, this is not going well."

The laughter subsided and one of them ventured the idea that this creature was not a real threat to them. He decided that a more diplomatic approach could move the encounter to a comfortable level.

"Allow me to introduce myself," he said with a smile. "My name is Finnegan and my friends call me Finny."

"You say you're a goat, but you don't look like us. You're bigger, and your fur is short and black. And I simply love those long loppy grey ears. By the way, in case you haven't noticed.....you don't have horns like we do. Are you sure you're a.....a goat?"

When Finny said "goat," he added a snooty head flip and the laughter renewed. Maria joined their fun-making and that made all the difference. The wall of tension crumbled.

"Yes, Finnegan, I am descended from a tribe of Nubian goats. My horns were removed when I was a baby and I've never given the lack of them any thought. It didn't matter until you mentioned it. Does that help?"

Finnegan responded: "Yeah, I guess it does."

"Going by what we just went through, I am supposing that you are goats too," said Maria with growing confidence. "What is your tribe?"

"I know there are other kinds of goats" stated

Finny, uncertain how to answer the question. "We've always lived in this valley for as long as the stories tell it. There are mountain goats that come through here from time to time. They look a lot like us, but their horns are a little smaller. And once, a couple of big horns showed up in the valley. Wow, do they have amazing horns. But they said they are sheep, not goats. I just don't know....."

"I think I can clear up the tribe issue," interrupted one of the others. "We are Angora goats; descendants of the ancient Alpine Ibex.....And my name is Tanny. What's yours?"

"My name is Maria, Tanny.

Maria turned to the third goat in the trio and asked about a name.

"My name is Rosie, Maria."

"And I know what it's like to be laughed at, too," Rosie giggled. "One of my horns broke when I was little and now it's grown in the strangest direction and makes me look funny. Plus, I'm smaller than the other girls. Sully calls me "special" in a loving sort of way, but Willie calls me names I don't want to repeat. He says it will make me tougher."

"Well I'm happy to meet another girl, Rosie. Who is your shepherd?

"If you don't mind me asking," queried Rosie. "What's a shepherd?"

"Oh my, let me think. What is a shepherd? Well,

I will do my best to tell you all what a shepherd is. Me and my sister, Carrie, have always had one; actually we have two. They are humans who take care of us, trim our hooves, feed us food and lead us to pastures where the best grasses are. Sometimes they take us to where there are some really yummy berry vines. At night they protect us and they keep us out of the rain and snow. They make noise but don't talk like we do. And....they are very nice."

It was obvious the description wasn't registering with the others. But Tanny looked like he was trying to remember something.

Rosie interjected: "We don't see humans very often. Willie tells us to stay away from them. So we do."

"I see," said Maria. And she thought it a good occasion to change the subject.

"My, my, you all have such beautiful long hair...... and your horns are curved so. Rosie, you're brilliant white.....like a wild rose?"

"We don't see wild roses around here very often, Maria," replied Rosie. "Although I have seen some, they usually get eaten before they open. But yes, that is why I have that name. Sully says I have a fragrant and sweet nature, like a wild white rose."

"Tanny, it would seem your color inspired your name," stated Maria. "And those curls are absolutely handsome."

Tanny shook his head a little. He was not accustomed to sincere compliments. "Ummmm, thank you."

The Visitor

"Tanny is our historian and storyteller," Rosie put in. "He knows all the old stories and keeps track of what happens from day to day. He's smarter than anybody and stays focused for such long periods of time when he's learning stuff."

Tanny took the statement as fact and acknowledged his office as storyteller with a modest "Yup."

More relaxed and confident to further her new acquaintances, Maria turned her attention to Finnegan.

"Finnegan, your color is just gorgeous!" she said almost gushing. "That long, straight fur is the most beautiful deep blue grey. I have never seen such color in any animal I have ever met.

"Perhaps I should tell you Finnegan's story," interjected Tanny. "It's a story that will be remembered for generations as I pass it on to the young ones." Without waiting for a response from the rest, he continued because he is the storyteller. And that is what storytellers do.

"As you may already know Maria, baby goats are often born at night in the worst of weather. Finnegan was no different in that respect. The night Finnegan arrived was severely cold with blowing wind filled with snow. After Finnegan's mother, Megan, gave birth, he struggled hard to stand up. But he couldn't. His legs were too weak. And it made it impossible for him to get milk."

"As the night wore into morning and the morning into day, Finnegan began to starve. Those early hours were so vital to his health. But he couldn't get up. Because of his growing weakness, Megan's milk didn't start. The day drew toward evening and we all gave up hope that Finnegan would live."

"Then something unusual happened. A human mysteriously appeared and picked up Finnegan in its arms. It held him for several minutes and mumbled words we could not understand. Then it put him down on his feet and held him steady until he could stand on his own. The visitor left as mysteriously as it came."

"The other mothers nursed him. From that time on he was well fed and grew. It seems the trouble he had in those first days affected his color in a rather extraordinary way. The old storyteller who was before me said it meant he was destined to do something great."

"If he doesn't grow impatient with the preparation process or become vain about his natural beauty, he will most likely be a fine leader when the rest of us are old or gone."

When Tanny finished with the story, Finnegan stood without speaking and feeling uneasy. Not because he was uncomfortable with being the focus of the story; he had grown to accept special notice as normal. But because the seeds of impatience and dissatisfaction had already been planted in his soul. He had been living with the weight of having to be the kind of person the leaders wanted him to be and had grown to resent the traditions and pressures of conformity being forced on him.

He wanted to be loved and accepted for the goat Finny knew was on the inside. But nobody really knew

The Visitor

that unique Finny. The exception would be his friend, Scampy. Unknown to Finny, not even he knew the complete identity of the real Finnegan. Yet, he wanted to be free of their pressures so he could explore and develop the uniqueness he wanted for himself.

"That's quite an interesting story," Maria said. "It's so unusual. Until recently, my life had been very ordinary."

On the wings of her statement, Maria related the story of how she ended up in their valley home. After she shared it all, nobody had an acceptable fix for her problem. It isn't odd among goats to have ready advice for fixing problems. But it is odd indeed to have no advice at all. Things just have to be fixed rather than let them be as they are.

Rosie suggested they all get a good drink, which is why they had come in the first place, then take Maria to meet the rest of the flock. All agreed it was a great idea and the four went their way chatting and laughing.

THE ENCOUNTER

By sunrise Roee had eaten enough for energy, put out the campfire, gathered his goods and set his focus on catching up with Maria.

He was puzzled about the lack of evidence that Maria had bedded down since the beginning of this tramp through the forest. Goats enjoy a respite after a good feed, then re-eat their food by chewing their cud. The rest time would have created a flattened area in the grasses if she had. But, there was nothing ordinary about this situation or this journey. Maria's disappearance was a source of growing wonderment.

A couple of hours into his odyssey, a creepy feeling nudged his senses that told him he wasn't alone. There had not been any sound to stir this feeling, just a sensitivity to his surroundings.

Up ahead a thick grove of manzanita posed an obstacle. He found a ten foot wide space Maria used to get through the dense growth. Once he was on the other side, he counted about twenty paces into a clearing. Back-stepping fifteen paces, he located a blind spot downwind from the trail where he could observe things while being hidden. Taking a large leap to the left, he exited the trail without leaving noticeable tracks or odor.

Taking position behind a large nearby tree, he withdrew the pistol from his holster and waited.

Feeling the pistol grip in his hand, he recalled what the angel said in his dream about new weapons. The words rang in his conscience: "You will no longer need the weapons of man, but the weapons and wisdom of the Kingdom of Heaven. Nothing will come between you and our Father's love. So do not be afraid. Be bold and courageous."

Roee has seen what a mountain lion or bear can do to weaker critters. There isn't a lot of protection in the strength of a man to ward off a mauling. "It would be over before it started," he considered.

Before he made his way through that thought, a mountain lion poked through the thicket and spied around. Seeing nothing, he sniffed the air and ventured into the clearing. When the puma committed to its exposure, the shepherd put away his gun and stepped from behind the tree. He took a brave confrontational stance with arms akimbo.

Among men and beasts mountain lions have little or nothing to fear. Wild marauders don't stalk them maliciously or seek them as a meal. When this man took his pose, the mountain lion simply sat down mystified. It didn't help his confidence that this human had a most peculiar smirk on his face.

The mountain lion considered......and rather snobbishly, "Hmmmm, he may not be as dumb as he looks."

Roee laughed and responded with the casual sarcasm of an old friend: "And you may not be as smart as you look young lion."

Understanding human speech for the first time was dumbfounding in no small way. Seeking to regain lost positional composure at the light-hearted jibe to his ego, he stood defiantly and took several steps toward Roee.

"How is it, you speak the language of my domain?" challenged the mountain lion.

"Maybe we should just call it a gift," rejoined the shepherd slowly.

The only "gift" this lion understood was an easy-to-catch meal, so the statement by-passed his comprehension and added the notion that this human was trying to make him look stupid. The response he rallied was an annoyed, "Yes, I see."

Roee kept the verbal edge to his advantage. "By the way, This is my Father's domain my fuzzy created one. He knows whether a heart is good or evil. And it is because of my Father that I understand what you say...... But tell me lion, what is your name? And why are you following me?"

"My name is Nara......at your service," replied the mountain lion arrogantly. Bouncing around in Nara's mind was the picture of following the shepherd in hopes of stealing the lost possession the shepherd was searching for. When the moment suited him, he will have a free feast to embrace or a human to hunt. But this knowledge needed to stay hidden, of course. He didn't answer the second question, but fielded what he hoped to be deflective questions. "And what is your name? And why would you be up here? Don't you live in the valley

The Encounter

below?"

"My name is Roee, and why I am here is of no concern to you." Pausing momentarily to study the cougar, he continued: "I believe you and I have met before."

Nara had made the acquaintance of several shepherds over the few years of his existence. Largely through the memory of the lingering human odor on goats and sheep he killed that belonged to them. Being upwind the scent could not register with a previous experience. Feigning innocence, he calmly lied: "You must be referring to my cousin, Leon."

"I will ask again........why are you following me?" persisted Rohee, discerning Nara was avoiding a direct answer.

Nara responded: "I am simply curious, Roee, and wondering why you would be this far from home. Perhaps you were lost or hunting for food. And there was the chance you might leave some morsel for me. As you know, nothing is wasted out here."

It was clear by the look on the shepherd's face he wasn't believing a word of Nara's story.

At first Roee smiled knowingly. Then his smile grew to a chuckle. Within a moment, he was on his way to all-out laughter. "If you were a scavenging bear, I could understand your thinking," retorted Rohee loudly. "But you're not. I think you have other intentions."

Nara had had enough of this ill-mannered and contemptuous chat. Nara's inflated opinion of himself had taken a beating during the course of it all and was ready to end it. But he chose to keep up a victim appearance.

Nara was used to being unchallenged and unafraid of anyone and anything. His supposed role of dominion in this forest, which he enforces with fear and bullying, works with weaker species. But this human, who put on airs of self-importance as an equal to him, was not intimidated and quite bothersome.

"You question my sincerity, Roee," stated Nara with an attempt to get Roee to drop his suspicious tone and take the dialogue in another direction. Control and manipulation are tools of his realm. Deceiving and lying advance his purposes.

Among his devices are schemes to get his prey believing he has good intentions. If the deception is believed, he persuades the unsuspecting victim to believe he is motivated to help them achieve their heart's desires. When his deception is complete, his quarry is captured in something else. Breaking their will and stealing the power of their dreams for his own gain, he laughs at their pain.

Encountering this shepherd will challenge the lion to reach deeper for a greater mastery.

"I know what you are, Nara. And there is no chance I will trust you," laughed Roee. "Your sincerity is no deeper than the bark on this tree."

Nara sneered, "If you didn't have those weapons, you and I would determine a great deal right here and now shepherd." He drew out the word shepherd and in that moment, revealed his true spirit.

Roee considered the words spoken by the angel that morning. As he understood, the new weapons he was looking for had not materialized. Their uncertain whereabouts left him wondering what they would be. But something was brewing in his thoughts.

He raised his shepherd's rod and spoke with authority. "I am a prince in the house of the Great King and a shepherd of the Chief Shepherd of all the earth!" stated Roee. "In Yeshua's name, I declare you have no part or place with me! Any advantage you think you have over me is an illusion! I live victoriously over you. You are no equal! I say You are already defeated and in the days ahead your dominion will fail at my word."

When Roee finished speaking, Nara was in a crouching position ready to spring on the shepherd. But he could not move. There was something to this human he could not fight. Yet, in his blindness and arrogance, he thought it better to be patient and wait for a better opportunity.

The conflict saturated the air with tangible gravity. Nara launched into the hole in the manzanita, leaving Roee to stand in the atmosphere of a new experience. He felt empowered and calmed by peace in the aftermath of his encounter.

Roee moved to a boulder nearby and sat with his knees to his forehead. His thoughts walked through the progression of possessing this new spiritual ground. Using a gun to end this encounter would have been easy. But choosing not to forced him to lay aside natural ways and draw from something greater.

Because of this conflict, he had a better understanding about the difference between the weapons he wore and the invisible ones given to fight spiritual battles. Natural weapons made him feel safe; they were familiar. But inside he suspected the day would come when ordinary weapons would not be as reliable as supernatural ones.

Practice and experience was Papa's way of preparing the shepherd for important encounters. The best teacher is real life and no greater instructor than a father's heart. Papa God is a good father. "No," said Roee affectionately, "You're the best father there is."

A smile simmered up from within, followed by the hum of a tune.

"In you my Father I put my trust

For you my King I raise a song of victory

With you my Lord I rule over my enemies

And humble those who rise against me"

"Show me your paths Papa teach me your ways

Reveal your truth and instruct me

Prepare my hands and heart for war

The Encounter

So I can stand next to you on those days"

"Great is your goodness my Shepherd

Great is your kindness my King

Great is your love my Lord

And great your power my Father"

While he praised, he found Maria's prints and continued his journey. Setting his happy heart to seeking the things that lay ahead, he sang as he hiked.

"You are good,

Giving love to generations

You are good

Giving life to the nations

You are good

You are goooooooood."

The two alpha bucks rose on their hind legs. Facing each other, they crashed horn to horn as they came down. The percussive crack reverberated off the surrounding rock monoliths.

"I'm taking it, you moron!" shouted Willie.

"It's mine, I found it!" rejoined Sully defiantly.

"I'm the head of this flock, and I'll take whatever I please!" bawled Willy in his typical crusty belligerence.

"You just think you're the head of this flock, and no! You will not take what you please!"

Rearing, the two made ready to bash heads again. A young kid had been watching the two seasoned fighters go at it with scheming interest. He rushed into the skirmish and grabbed the wild apple in his mouth and scurried off, kicking his feet in victory.

Sully yelled as he came down: "Scampy, you'll pay for this!"

Willy bellowed with laughter, "Atta boy, son!"

Scampy stopped a safe distance away and munched the stolen prize through muffled chuckles.

Life in Wonder Valley is best described as semi-unruly. Even with traditions, understandings of protocol and rules created to control and prevent rather than empower, hope is a marginal value that is offset by longings for better days. Advancement away from the love of rules is slow for lack of wisdom about how to rule with love.

This conundrum makes everyday life messy, chaotic and uncertain giving place to discontent. There is an idiom stated and repeated often among these goats, "It's a wonder anyone can stay sane in this valley." Thus the name, Wonder Valley.

An inherent nature in goats makes them uniquely

The Encounter

suited for these wilderness surroundings. Balance refers not only to their natural stability, but their emotional equilibrium as well. Collectively dysfunctional with occasional tragedies, mild indifference seems to make it manageable.

Not everyone has fallen prey to that indifference. Those who resist it, face continual occasion for argument, injustice and strong opinion to answer against them. Its frustrations make caring goats keep silent rather than face verbal horn-buttings.

On the other hand, it is amazing to behold the diplomatic skills learned by those who act and speak on behalf of the goodwill of others. The crucial ingredient is a never give up attitude.

Like Willie said, he is the supposed leader of the goats. That presumptive position happened because he's strong and intimidating. Over the years, he's won the most battles over food and companionship. For that reason alone, he has fathered a lot of the flock.

While he maintains a steeled outward persona with strong opinions, tenderness and tolerance leak out periodically. It is reflected in his handling of Scampy.

Scampy got his name through his constantly playful nature and energetic scampering over rocks, logs, other goats and any climbing thing he could find. Although a yearling, he is revealing qualities as a future leader of the flock. Whoever gains influence over his undeveloped character will form Scampy's budding leadership.

Willie and Sully carry the bulk of genuine concern

for the flock. Their values are often polarized between optimism and negativity, with practical results falling somewhere in the middle.

His nickname is Sully because Sullivan was too formal to be used by a goat flock. It felt like there should have been a "mister" in front of it; like Mister Sullivan. The moniker simply didn't fit.

Sully has a distinctively noble virtue; the fortitude of having the hide of an alligator and the heart of a dove. In less figurative words, he faces considerable bashings by others and remains steadfastly gentle.

Opinions and insults roll off, effectively keeping him as a person of influence. Although his patience wears thin when his buttons get intentionally pushed---- Willy being the prime culprit.

Sully's an advocate and fights back on behalf of the flock for justice, compassion and tolerance.

Being one of the alpha leaders, he has strong opinions with practical and objective viewpoints without the selfishness and short-sightedness that can be the substance of opinion. Willy and the others call them "goatisms."

Although imperfectly, he puts things across sensibly for the good of the many. That doesn't mean his goatisms prevail. But his ideas are heard and have their place and timing in nurturing and creating a future for the flock.

Tanny is the third of the leaders. Storytelling is his

heritage; he was prepared for it from kidhood. In this flock, storytellers are the historians who track events, changes, losses and traditions. Tanny has refined his craft to a science. He makes his stories interesting, easy to remember and leaves his listeners wanting more.

Like Rosie said, he's smart and keenly aware of how his responsibilities work within the flock. In his estimation, if it were not for remembering the past, there would be no point of reference for their future.

The Meeting

The watering haven Maria found when she first arrived is accessed at the end of a corridor of meadow. As if nature had created it for that purpose, the small pond is fed by the creek as it runs through and provides a safe zone under the tree limbs.

Returning from there, Tanny, Finny, Rosie and Maria walked the middle of the meadow toward the crook in the dogleg. Getting beyond the turn, they headed toward the group competing for the wild apple.

Maria's arrival created no small stir with the flock. Heads turned in curiosity. Others who were busy grazing lifted their eyes. Small groups pulled together to whisper their suspicions. What was coming toward them? But none approached the four to ask about their visitor.

Willie blurted out rudely: "Who are you and what do you want?"

Rosie stepped forward to intercede and make introductions.

"This is our new friend, Maria," Rosie began. "And she is..."

"I'll let you know if she's going to be a friend, Rosie," interrupted Willie. "And she is what?"

Keeping a respectful tone, Rosie continued. "She is a Nubian goat, sir. And she is lost and we need to help her somehow."

"Young nanny, how can we help you if you don't know where you came from?" responded Willie gruffly.

"For goodness sake, Willie," injected Sully. "Where's your heart? There's no reason to be rude. She's not a threat to anybody. "

"Look at her, Sully, she's different," barked Willie. "Her fur's different, her color's different, she doesn't have any horns and she even............ She even smells different. She can't be trusted!"

"You can't judge by appearances, Willie. What really matters is on the inside."

"Keep your goatisms, Sully. I'll make up my own mind about this."

Tanny stepped up with a softer approach.

"The traditions tell us," he started, "that we decide these things as a group. We had a talk with her, and she's a very nice goat."

"Your silly traditions.....bah!" grumbled Willie. "She probably listened to one of your stories, Tanny. That's why you like her."

"Enough, Willie!" said Sully impatiently. Sighing, he continued, "Please tell us about your situation, Maria."

Maria composed herself. She had never known

prejudice and it upset her. Her world was filled with love and protection by her shepherds. This incident so unnerved her she wasn't sure she wanted to talk.

Rosie broke the silence with: "Go ahead, Maria. Willie's prickly on the outside, but tender on the inside. That's one of Sully's sayings."

Bleats from the older female goats registered disapproving votes on Rosie's report. But Rosie's statement encouraged Maria to venture into this chaotic culture and take whatever came.

"I remember," started Maria, "being at home in the morning with my sister Carrie. I don't know what happened, but the next thing I remember is hearing loud laughter and finding myself not too far from the creek. It was so strange. I just don't know how I got here! After that I found my way to the water for a drink and ran into these three. It's not much of a story is it?"

"I don't believe it!" jumped in Willie. "I think you're spying on us."

"Why would she do that?" challenged Scampy.

"Because we have enemies, boy," stated Willie impatiently. "You're much too young to understand these things. Just listen to me."

"We don't have enemies that are goats, Willie," retorted Sully, feeling impatience rise again.

"Look, there's always the possibility of the first time. Let's not get over-confident about these things,

Sully," replied Willie defensively.

"You're impossible...," sighed Sully. He shook his head and rolled his eyes to show his annoyance.

As he did that, he noticed movement in the corridor toward the water haven. His eyes magnetically landed on a human walking their direction. A man smiling broadly, wearing a large brimmed straw hat, green plaid flannel shirt, denim jeans and a number of strange things sticking here and there around him.

"What could this possibly be?" He wondered to no one in particular. Everyone turned to see what he was looking at.

Maria recognized him.

"It's my shepherd!" she said breathlessly; astonished to think she would be rescued so soon.

"I told you!.....She's a spy! Look what she's brought here!," jumped in Willie loudly.

"Stop it, Willie," rejoined Sully. "Do you even know what a shepherd is? I don't."

"No, but it can't be good," said Willie suspiciously. "Remember, it's a human!"

"There's things about them in the old, old stories, Willy" considered Tanny. "Some of them were like heroes."

Maria ran toward the shepherd, her excitement unrestrained.

Roee laughed aloud and yelled her name: "Maria! Oh my precious Maria!"

When he spoke, Maria's eyes widened and she tried skidding to a stop, ending with a slide into his strong arms as he stooped to enfold her. She recognized the laughter from her awakening in the forest.

"I must be having a dream!" she told herself. Her head and heart spun dizzily.

"This is no dream, Maria," responded Roee.

"You can talk!" she said as a question and a statement. "I can understand what you're saying!"

"I know, isn't that amazing?" added Roee with a warm smile.

Several goats in the flock gathered around in wonderment. They were curious yet ready to run at the first sign of a problem. Tanny the storyteller stood among them with the expectation of an unfolding story.

"What happened?" asked Maria. "How is it we can talk to each other? This....is so....This is so special. But that doesn't say enough. This is a miracle!"

The shepherd rose, then stroked behind her ears affectionately.

"It's a truly wild story. And I'll be happy to share the whole thing with you shortly," said Roee. "But first, who are these new friends of yours?"

"We're not friends yet, mister," said Willie, trying

to crush the friendship idea and determined to be watch-ful.

"Willie stop," said Sully. "You're being positively rude!"

"I would like to hear your story," interjected Tanny with hopeful determination. "I certainly would indeed."

Maria took a breath, gathered her wits and made introductions.

"This is Tanny, shepherd. He is the tribe historian and storyteller."

"Well then, Tanny, you shall certainly hear the story of my wondrous journey. My name is Roee."

"That's a beautiful name." exclaimed Maria.

Maria gave the names of those brave enough to come close. Wild goats are cautious and even fearful for what seems like no reason. But, everyone in their own time would discover the shepherd to be a safe person.

When the rounds brought the introductions to Willie, he went right to the matter on his heart.

"Why are you here and where are you from?" de-manded Willie directly.

Roee held no offense toward Willie. He knew Wil-lie was looking out for the good of the flock in the only way he understood. In his spirit though, he perceived there was a deeper question brewing in Willie.

The shepherd didn't know it, but the old traditions

of the tribe had become a source of emptiness and frustration for Willie. Over time, he lost hope of any happiness and turned grumpy about his lot in life. He stuck it out and did what was expected of him. But, the sense of duty left him unfulfilled and unhappy.

The unspoken question at the core of Willy's being was: "Is this all there is?" His discontent rendered him critical of everything and judgmental of everyone. The mindset drained him of affection. And if the truth were told, Willie was lonely. Even in this crowd of goats, he felt alone. But he could never tell anyone. It would mark him as weak.

"I've been searching for my Maria for three days since I left Grindlay Village," responded Roee to Willie's question calmly. "It's down the mountain from here." He pointed then said, "In that direction."

"Maria is your possession?" said Willie in disbelief. "That's disgusting!"

"Willie, it's a term of endearment!" Roee responded. "Maria and I have a mutually beneficial, loving and happy relationship. She and her sister Carrie provide good things for us. We provide good things and protection for them. And we have fun doing it."

"Love?" said Willie, softening just slightly. "Happy?" The words didn't really have a meaning that he had an experience for. "Humph. I wouldn't know about those kinds of things......Fun?"

Roee smiled, then looked around for ways he could tangibly express examples of "those kinds of things."

"What do you do to protect the flock from the cold, rain and snow up here?" he asked.

Willie looked around and said, "We take refuge under tree limbs in the rain and behind big rocks when the cold wind blows."

"As you might suspect," said Willie sarcastically, "goats aren't equipped to build things."

Roee started to laugh, but thought better of it because of the serious look on Willie's face.

"So many of our newborns die in the freezing nights," said Willie sadly. "I have often wondered why the does have their babies in the coldest and craziest weather. It makes it hard for the young ones to survive."

As Willie grew pensive, he caught himself being drawn into trusting this stranger. He reconsidered and decided against it.

"Now that you have found Maria, I suppose you will be leaving," he stated with a hard edge in his voice.

"If it's okay with you and the others, we could stay a few days and make a couple shelters for the flock. Talking with Tanny about your history would be fantastic fun. And I could share my own stories with anyone who wanted to hear them."

"I don't know about that," said Willie warily. "If you have any harm in mind, you'll find the point of a goat horn not to your liking."

"Fair enough Willie" rejoined Roee without flinching. "I would protect my flock with the same resolve."

That statement caught Willie's attention. But he tucked his observation away to wait and see what actions were behind the words.

Roee walked away as Willie considered this human. He had not known any before and had never heard about one that could talk. Those who traveled through this valley in the past showed little concern for them. Some old stories told of humans hunting them for food. But this human was different. Willie could understand what he was saying. And why should this guy be concerned for the well-being of goats he hardly knew?

Roee had a calming influence. Being around him stilled the tension in Willie's soul. "I really can't figure that out at all," Willie thought.

"A shepherd. What the heck is a shepherd?" muttered Willie to himself. "What do the old stories say about that?"

Overhearing, Tanny interrupted Willie's jumbled and reflective musings.

"I can help you with that question, Willie," said Tanny with confidence.

Questions and answers oscillated back and forth until Willie couldn't process any more information. He would think about things for awhile and put the parts together. Then, he would have more questions.

"We will talk again later Tanny," he concluded.

The Meeting

By evening Roee had walked a tour of the the valley and made an analysis of simple things that could be added to make flock life more comfortable.

There was time for chatting with more goats as some lost their wariness of him. Others still found it awkward to wrap their horns around the idea a talking human.

"It'll come with time," he presumed and set about finding a suitable place to sleep for the night. But before finishing the day, he determined to find time with Maria.

Roee knew Maria was occupied with her new friends and caught up in particular with the fun of newborns. These little fluffs of cuteness and energy were constant entertainment.

He found Maria standing with Rosie watching the little ones frolic. The two were busy laughing and talking as Roee approached from the side.

The shepherd spotted what they were taken up with; a tree leaning against another at an apex about fifteen feet from the ground. Several kids had climbed up a thirty foot length of the trunk and were lined up one behind the other. Butting and pushing, they jostled for better positions.

"That looks scary." stated Roee, "Won't the kids get hurt playing these games?"

"It's through these play times," responded Rosie,

"that we learn balance and gain strength. It might look dangerous, but it's an important part of a goats' growing up."

Roee reflected on that statement then said, "Humans often avoid risk and danger because it's safe. I can see where we could learn faith, courage and teamwork by taking risks. We could discover something from these children."

After a short pause he added, "But I think I need a different set of feet for something like that." Roee chuckled at his attempt to be funny. The girls smiled, rolled their eyes and looked at each other good-naturedly.

Regardless of their response, the humor allowed him access to their moment in a gentle way. And having gained it, he shared why he had come.

"The sun will be setting shortly and I told Maria I would tell her how I came to have this gift of talking to animals. Rosie, you are welcome to join us, but I would like to move toward where I'm sleeping tonight. Is that okay?"

As the three of them walked and talked, Roee asked Maria to describe her journey to the valley.

She repeated her account for the shepherd as goats hanging around the area started to follow. The number mounted not because of the story, but because it's just what goats do.

Questions and stories were the social center piece for the remainder of the evening. Starting with his

dream about the angel, then his encounter with the
raccoon family, Roee established the moment of impartation of his gift. With the small ones around he knew
he should wait for a more appropriate time to tell of his
showdown with Nara.

Tanny shared stories at Roee's request. There was a
lengthy but interesting account of the history of the tribe
and their ancestry with the Alpine Ibex. He retold the
chronicle for Roee's sake of Finnegan's birth and tales
of mysterious disappearances, like Finnegan's mother
Megan. Tanny's masterful storytelling kept time flowing
without notice.

The sun was gone and a sliver of a moon smiled its
minimal light. The goats didn't move about after dark
for lack of nocturnal vision. The place was pleasant with
warm bodies and sleep came easy.

At first light, Roee was off for a walk with Papa
to find suitable materials to make shelters. His hatchet
made quick work of cutting poles from tree limbs. Starting with live trees near the meadow for uprights, he created pitched roofs with joists high enough to keep young
goats from climbing on top. He thatched the shelters
using pine boughs to shed rain and sun until he could
resource a better solution.

While building, work was often interrupted with
chats. Willie, Sully and Tanny dropped by frequently,
curious about the outside world and asking questions
about Roee's existence. Roee's questions usually provoked

a story or two from Tanny. Others came by to socialize and laugh it up during the day.

Mid afternoon of the third day, the shepherd wrapped up his project.

He was longing to rejoin his wife and certain she was worried about his absence. He set a departure time for the following morning.

Finding Sully, he shared his plans.

"I think we should pull the flock together for a talk about this. Your friendship is important and we'd like to give you a proper goat sendoff."

"It would do my heart good," responded Roee, "to be a part of that."

"We'll come find you later."

Roee ventured into the forested north hills in search of a place he could be alone to meditate and enjoy a view from higher up. He ascended a rock mass and found a flat table-like area at the top where he sat reflecting on the six days of this adventure. It encouraged him that each day had been pleasantly touched by the hand of Papa.

Roee had grown accustomed to looking for God's love language and his heart was trained to be watchful for the small things Papa used to commune with him and leave notes for him to discover. Lately, those notes expanded into notices of life-change. They tested him to hear and respond swiftly. Roee deeply appreciated the challenges because it was Papa's way of showing him trust.

Considering what his new assignment might be created uncertainties. On the one hand, were these wild goats his destination? On the other hand, would Dodee leave the home she had worked hard to put together to be a part of this tribe?

Rocc kncw thc King's ways. Hc could rcst confidant that Papa was aware of both hands and everything would be handled well by him. Striving would serve no purpose and only hinder getting Papa's instructions clearly.

Assuring peace replaced concern as Roee settled into communion with his God. Tranquility gave way to a dream-like atmosphere and natural surroundings disappeared. Music crescendoed in the background and Heaven opened before him.

Music staffs and notes whorled from the mouth of a conch-shaped amphitheater. They ricocheted off the stone ledge in front of him, flying ribbon-like in different directions. Flowing high, long and wide around the valley, they wove among trees and bushes, and penetrated the stream and the stone formations. One staff spun into a flock of geese resting in the meadow, scattering them playfully. Notes from the staves removed themselves, hiding and embedding. Every living note, even the rests and stops, carried and deposited life.

Without bass or treble clef on the staves, the notes achieved pitches beyond the natural hearing. High notes embraced then bounced off tips of trees, intertwining with limb and leaf. Low notes rumbled under large boulders then geysered to envelop clouds above. Mid tones danced gracefully on the surface of the stream, chorused joyously among the meadow's grasses then boomed drum-like with cliffs above the forest.

The symphonic storm swashed its spontaneous opera with non-mortal instruments, to be heard by an applauding creation eagerly awaiting its song. The music score was sovereignly written for the valley where the transformational overture was orchestrated. Roee was caught up in the masterpiece from intimate chambers deep in his being and sung along with a language that flowed like the current of a deep river.

Roee saw himself leave the stone ledge and went singing into the trees, the water, the dirt, the cliffs; everything in the valley. He sung life into every creature and prepared a way for those that would someday come, called by an unseen beckoning.

The song echoed off the mountains and cliffs, adding reverberation and substance. The front ends of the now empty staffs returned from their journey through the valley. They swirled together in upward motion then disappeared like an upside down tornado back into the amphitheater. All was peaceful and quiet as the last notes harmonically sustained. Roee watched the conclusion as the heavenly stage drew up and faded. Sent by God it now returned to him, having accomplished what it was sent to do. Heaven had kissed earth with a new song of life.

His heart pounded with excitement as he made a panoramic scan of the valley. For a few moments, Roee's vision was not earthly. Then as he watched, his new friends gathered below, having only heard his one-man song.

He came down from the rock and headed for the meadow.

Sully commented as Roee approached the group, "That was quite a song."

"My heart goes to amazing places when God is present," responded Roee. "Perhaps I could teach you guys to sing," added the shepherd with a chuckle.

As they laughed with him, someone asked: "Who ever heard of goats singing?"

"Let's try a choir of goats.....Come on everybody," led Roee, "give me be your best bahs and bleats. Ready?....One, two, three, four." With that he brought down his hand to cue them to start, counted several bars with his arms then held out his arms maintaining a decent sustaining end. Roee went to the cut and brought his arms and fingers together.

Along with the few words that could possibly describe what happened next, heaven was smiling broadly. The harmonies were incredible....incredibly off. And their unabashed enthusiasm was worth the price of the ticket, as they say.

Guffaws of laughter arose until a pile of hoof and horn joined the shepherd. Bonds of friendship completed their formation.

As the laughter waned Roee stated with feigned sincerity, "With a little practice, I think y'all can be famous." This started another round of merriment with added "oh yeah" and "sure thing" mingled in.

Even Willie captured the mood of the moment. "I haven't laughed like that," he breathed heartily, "since I was young and ornery.....Thanks, Roee....Sully says, you're heading home tomorrow morning."

"I'm sure my wife is worried about my whereabouts; I've been gone longer than we expected."

"You've brought a lot to the atmosphere of this valley in the short time you've been here. We really don't want to see you go. In fact we want to invite you to come back as often as you like. Maybe you could even come back and live here. What do you say?"

Roee looked at every face and they looked back in anticipation of his response.

He smiled and said honestly: "I would like that very much and I'm confident we will come back and visit. But my wife needs to prepare herself if she is to leave there and come here. It's part of being a silly human.....That may not be the answer you want. But it is the best answer I have today. Things could change. There is the God factor to consider. Can you guys accept that for now?"

"We are thankful that you would consider honoring us with another visit," said Sully. "How long would you be gone?"

"Perhaps by the next full moon we could make our way back."

"That isn't very long," rejoined Willie.

The others added their affirmations.

The shepherd had a thought come to mind and briefly considered how to say it.

"Do you know that Nara is in the vicinity?" seeing this as an opportunity to bring the alert. "I ran into him on the way here."

"I haven't heard of anyone seeing him until now," said Willie.

"It's usually too late when you do hear about it, Willie," replied Roee. "He's sneaky, quiet and a patient hunter."

Everyone nodded in agreement.

"Pass the word to the others to be watchful and stay together......I love you guys."

Now that was a new one that caught the guys off guard. They weren't quite sure how to respond. So, only a couple of "thank you" were heard in return. Being loved was new to them.

"Would you mind telling me more about your encounter with Nara?" requested Tanny.

A Shift In Time

In the twilight of the morning of his departure Roee was back at the rock ledge where he experienced the previous day's vision. His heart was set on some time to meditate and listen.

The call given him in the dream his first night away from the village had gained clarity with each day since. What decisions that needed to be made were obvious. If left with his own counsel he would present the call around strong points of purpose. His points would be compelling and convincing. He could draw Dodee's heart toward embracing whatever picture he presented.

But to do it that way would be manipulation and Papa would not be pleased.

Before retiring the night before he had given Dodee a lot of thought. He cared about her heart and didn't want her to feel her time at Grindlay Village was wasted. He would be asking her to give up all they had been building together.

His plan would need patience and tenderness, so he couldn't strive in any fashion. What they have is a three-way partnership with Papa. Her response will establish the atmosphere of the next season of their lives and it had to be right.

It occurred to him there would be opportunity to

A Shift In Time

have Maria as a sounding board during their return journey. That reasoning sounded hollow, but it might be fun to hear what she had to say.

Papa interrupted his train of thought with, "Just tell her about the gift and the goats, nothing more."

Within minutes of returning to camp, Roee gathered everything he needed. Maria was still saying good-byes. He had said his and understanding Maria's nature, he didn't ask if she was ready. He simply stated, "It's time," and started walking. It only took a minute for her to figure out he was not waiting and that his statement was not an advanced warning. She caught up easily.

Given that the journey home was downhill, the shepherd calculated two full days to arrive home...maybe two and a half.

Approaching the manzanita's dense grove, the shepherd considered it cautiously. His ears and other senses were alert for trouble. He made note that it needed safer passage through and he should rectify the problem someday.

Beyond the hazardous part, their pace picked up nicely. Hours into their hike, they came to the place where Roee encountered the raccoon family and where he laughed for the longest time. Maria marveled about hearing his laughter through the great distance lying between these two points. It was his laughter that had broke her "enchantment."

He retold details so she could coordinate the account with events in her memory, bookmarking where Roee had received the dream and the activation of the gift.

Maria suggested giving the place a name. A few attempts produced little inspiration as they couldn't think of anything suitable. Roee proposed waiting and added, "It was the moment that was special, not necessarily the place. We'd probably lose track of it in time anyway."

Maria continued, "I'm really looking forward to sharing our stories with Carrie and Mama Shepherd when we get back."

Maria had a puzzled look on her face. "You think Mama Shepherd can talk to animals like you do?"

Roee looked at her, amused he hadn't thought of it before. He observed how quickly he had adjusted to his new normal. "No she doesn't," he said chuckling. "But I know Papa will include her in this blessing somehow. It'll be fun to see how he does it."

He smiled at her and drank in the moment they were sharing. "I can just see her now, Maria," he continued. "Oh, is she going to laugh."

After a pause he said, "We're making good time. It's so much easier going downhill."

"I wouldn't know," laughed Maria. "I don't remember."

With the sun rapidly approaching the horizon,

Roee told Maria he wanted to slow the pace and watch for a place to bed down for the night.

Maria had a different proposal.

"I still have lots of energy," she stated enthusiastically. "Can we keep going a little longer?"

"Well, we still have another hour or so before nightfall," he said. "Sure, I'm good for that much. Great idea Maria!"

They headed on briskly and chatted at length about how they could form their stories the way Tanny did.

They lost track of time and light while they hiked and made conversation, oblivious to their surroundings. The shepherd noticed a clearing in the undergrowth and trees up ahead that looked like an archway.

"I don't remember that being here," Roee grumped to himself. "I hope I didn't get us lost!"

Stopping at the opening in the arch, Roee looked beyond then took off his hat.

"This....this isn't possible!" he declared, staggered by what he saw.

"Dodee, Carrie, we're home!" he yelled excitedly.

Response from the house was immediate as sounds of things falling to the floor rang from within. The door to the cabin flung open and Dodee stepped onto the porch. She put her hands on her hips and shook her head in mock disapproval of his absence. But her growing smile told a different story.

In the span of time from the crash on the floor to Dodee standing on the porch, Roee had run the distance from the archway and scooped her into his arms.

"I am so glad to see you."

Dodee watched Carrie and Maria playfully butt heads in affection and bleat their greetings.

"Did you have any trouble while I was gone?" asked Roee.

"Papa's presence took care of me while you were away," Dodee replied confidently. "I knew everything would be alright."

Smiling, she shook her finger in his face. "But that didn't keep me from wondering what was taking you so darned long. What happened?"

"Ohhhh, we do have some stories to tell, my love."

Dodee looked at him quizzically, then around the area. "We? Did you bring somebody home with you?"

With a look of knowing something she didn't, he said: "Just Maria....Could we catch up over something to eat? I'm starved. I've been living off the wilds all this time."

Dodee looked into his eyes and smiled again. "Welcome home love, come on in."

_____

A Shift In Time

For the next hour, the two cooked a hot meal to share and sat down with a small fire in the fireplace to overcome a chill from the spring evening.

Roee opened his journal, and carefully narrated the adventures of his journey. He told about the dream and his encounter with the raccoon family and left room for Dodee to ask questions.

"Let me see if I got this right," she said with one eyebrow raised and her head slightly cocked to one side. "You can carry on conversations with animals?"

"Yes I can. And as far as I can tell, any animal that is willing to chat. I haven't tested everybody, like fish and birds and stuff. But I'm pretty sure it's everything. I'd really like to see how it works with horses and dogs."

"That could be really handy. Do I have your permission to ask you to interpret for me when the goats are being contrary?" She couldn't help but laugh at what she said. And neither could Roee.

"I am your humble animal language interpreter, madam. At your service.....Large or small, I do them all. Day or night, I get it right."

A river of affection runs sweetly through Roee and Dodee's relationship, leaving little room for distrust or insecurity. And there is always respectful space for playful digs at the other's expense.

"You know what?" declared Dodee confidently. "I may not need you to interpret for me."

"Why is that?" responded Roee in fake disappointment.

"Because Papa is a good, good father and I am his favorite," she said in playful tones. "He's so generous with us, Roee. I will simply ask him for the same thing so we can do it together."

"That would be beautiful," marveled Roee.

"Now, tell me more."

Leaving out the part where Papa spoke to him about their calling with the wild goats, he shared his encounter with the mountain lion and his finding Maria amongst the flock. He told about their differences and their animated personalities.

The fire burned as he shared until Dodee reached the end of her listening capacity. Agreeing to continue the account after a good night's sleep, they drifted into small talk, cleaning dishes and eventually wandering to a warm bed.

Dodee and Roee threw themselves into morning routines rested and with purpose. Roee was off to see Papa's face in the colors of the sunrise, while Dodee preferred to see him through a comfortable chair and the warmth of a fireplace.

On his way back, Roee checked in with Maria and Carrie.

Maria told Carrie about the shepherd's ability to

A Shift In Time

talk with animals the day before. But Carrie was still unprepared for the real thing.

"Good morning Maria," Roee began with a smile.

"And, a pleasant morning to you Carrie. I'm sorry I didn't get out to talk with you last night. But the evening simply got full with chatting it up with Mama Shepherd........Aren't you glad to have Maria back?"

"Oh my," stated Carrie in wonder. "It is so strange to understand what you're saying."

"I've talked to you many times in the past," rejoined Roee in playful surprise. Not waiting for a response, he continued. "Did Maria tell you about how it happened?"

"I told her so many stories," interrupted Maria. "We talked until we couldn't talk anymore."

Laughing aloud, the shepherd roared: "Is such a thing even possible?"

Carrie added giggling, "You have a marvelous sense of humor."

"Not bad for a goatman, eh?" retorted the shepherd.

Having heard the chatter outside, Dodee slipped away from the cabin and approached quietly from behind. What she heard was unsurprisingly different than what Roee was hearing.

"It is so bizarre," she interrupted while scratching the twins behind the ears, "to watch you talk to the girls like they understand you and have them bleat their responses......This will require some adjustments."

"Not only do I understand them," responded Roee, "but I identify with them like I do with you. Any animal can become friend, foe or undecided; just like people. I can be considerate of their feelings and discern their intentions and relate with them on the level Papa created them.......When I was in the mountains with the flock, it became normal to talk as you and I do."

Dodee observed Roee's face while he talked. It revealed a depth about him that had not been there before.

Roee was always a good caretaker of the natural environment around the farm and forest. Dodee shares in this devotion for the out-of-doors. Although he hunts and fishes for food, he respects the animal world that makes their home around them. The farm is a sanctuary for wild creatures as long as they stay out of the vegetable garden. But something had impacted Roee while he was gone. Knowing he would reveal it in his time, she decided to wait and watch.

Dodee had been looking around casually since his last statement.

"I'm not ignoring you, love. I'm just thinking about a few of the chores that stacked up while you were gone. How about I fix breakfast while you're working on them. What do you say to that?"

He smiled and said, "I sure missed you and your cooking. That sounds wonderful."

"I'll come get you when it's ready." With a hug and

a kiss, they got on with the day.

While Roee worked through the chores.......cleaning the chicken coop, splitting fire wood and watering where needed........he looked around and analyzed how he would manage to move everything a three day trek through the forest. Not seeing any roads near the upper valley, it would be a massive endeavor for just the two of them to pull off.

He considered the idea of using a small army of goats as beasts of burden, like one uses donkeys or mules to carry things. In reflecting on their independence and tendency to wander, he laughed and put the idea aside.

He thought he would try out his new gift on the chickens. His first attempt proved unproductive. They ran screaming into the coop in mortal terror and refused further dialogue, confirming that clear communication cannot overcome the silliness and stupidity of chickens.

With Carrie and Maria tagging along and grazing, they had opportunity to share in the shepherd's comic relief with the dramatic chickens.

Their presence afforded Roee the occasion to talk with Carrie about how she fared while Maria was away.

"She's never disappeared like that before. We've always been together. We were having a simply normal morning and suddenly she was gone. When you left later, I knew there was a problem. But, when you didn't come back the next day, I cried. After four days, I lost hope that either of you were coming back."

"Why four days, Carrie?" asked Roee.

"Because I only have four hooves," she laughed. "That's as much as I can count."

Roee grabbed her head at the ears and shook her playfully. They laughed as he knuckle-bumped them both above their eyes. Roee was satisfied that the animals were in good emotional shape.

As he headed toward the wood pile to do some splitting, Dodee hollered that breakfast was on the table.

Entering the cabin, Roee immediately felt Papa's presence and a warm glow from his beloved. Something special was going on.

There was more story to be told about the last several days and a lot to consider as to why there was now a story. Without feeling rushed, Roee thought it best to stay in the moment and let their talk flow naturally.

As Dodee laid the plates gently on the table, she didn't need words to show Roee she was comforted by them being back together. Their eyes met in warm assurance of two hearts well connected. Their dozen years together had produced depth and tenderness that could not be derailed by unusual circumstances.

After Roee gave thanks to Papa for the meal, he looked at Dodee and seeing she was thoughtful, asked what was on her heart.

"I was watching you and the girls talk outside," she

began as she sat down. "It was cute seeing you treat them like they were your daughters. I see beauty in the gift you've been given........When I considered what a good father you would be, it just warmed me inside to think about it. Then the warmth kept growing and spread through me as I was thankful for Papa bringing you home safely."

"His presence felt like oil flowing over me and I heard Papa say very clearly, "My child, you will have sons and daughters in the years to come. Some will come from your own womb. By this time next year, you will be carrying a baby girl in your arms."

As she finished the account of her encounter, Roee lay down his fork and put his hands over his heart. His eyes moist with tears, he reached across the table and took her hands.

"We have an amazing life together, my love. That is precious news."

Breakfast will be cold but still appreciated by the time they get back to it. But for this moment, a feast of a different sort would be shared first.

The two shepherds enjoyed the afternoon in the sunshine. Dodee tended the vegetable garden while Roee split firewood.

After her chore was done, Dodee approached Roee from the garden.

Smiling, she asked, "Are you about done?"

"I can quit anytime. Is there something you need me to do?"

"I have an idea I would like you to consider."

"Whatever you desire.....even to half my kingdom," he responded with a genteel bow at the waist and exaggerated sweep of his arms.

She hooked her hand behind his sweaty elbow and steered him to where Carrie and Maria were grazing. As they strolled, she began, "While I was in the garden, I was trying to visualize your friends up on the mountain, and not doing it successfully."

"I have not described them very well, I think," Roee interrupted, trying to fix the problem. "I can tell you more about them."

"That would be good," she responded patiently. "But I have a suggestion that might be a little better. What would you think of the four of us going there for a visit?"

Roee was not expecting her request and looked at her like a deer in the headlights. Misreading his expression, she continued.

"I know you just got back from there and it is such a long way to hike. It doesn't need to be right away so you could get rested and all. But this journey of yours is so full of wonders. I really would like to see it for myself. Could you give it some thought?"

A Shift In Time

Roee folded his arms on his chest, and settled his chin into the pocket of his thumb and index finger of his left hand. Appearing deep in thought as he looked intently into Dodee's eyes, a mischievous smile broadened across his face. He uncrossed his arms, turned to the girls and rested his hands on his hips.

"Carrie! Maria! How would you like to visit our new friends in the high country?"

Like an explosion, Maria was immediately giddy with leaping and prancing in excitement while Carrie looked on laughing.

Dodee didn't need an interpreter to understand the answer to that question.

"We could have Nate and Isaac look after the chickens, collect the eggs and water the garden for a couple of weeks," declared Roee. "Maybe you could make a couple of saddle-like bags for Carrie and Maria? They would be immensely helpful for carrying food and blankets."

"They won't be stylish," responded Dodee nodding slowly, "but they will be practical."

"Yay, we get to help!" exclaimed the girls, excited at the prospect of making the trip.

THE RETURN

Preparations for making a two week excursion invariably filled with more detail than expected. On the morning of the fifth day since Roee and Maria's return home the quartet headed back to Wonder Valley.

Two excited goats.....loaded with food, water and blankets......were keyed up with eager energy. Roee hoped they would hold steady for the three day trek. He felt that keeping them focused and entertained for the distance could prove challenging.

The uphill climb of the first day was serene and uneventful and not all that demanding. Yet a restorative rest from the exertion was welcomed long before night-fall. The upside was the shade of the forest. It kept them insulated from the warm spring sunshine and conserved their water. An occasional meadow provided the girls with graze time for energy boosts. Roee had built up endurance with his previous journeys through this terrain and was in good shape. But Dodee would discover an on-the-job physical makeover by trails end.

Repacked, fed and on their way by sunrise, the second morning was looking like a repeat of the first. By mid-afternoon, they arrived at the location where Roee had his dream and received his gift of talking with the animals.

It wasn't likely they would find the raccoon family during the day. But it was a good opportunity to share the dream and encounter with them in greater detail for Dodee and Carrie's sake. He showed them the tree of his raccoon encounter. The tracks they created were still visible. He pointed out where he made camp that night and completed the show part of his telling.

The mysterious and extraordinary happened here. Roee explained the place as a portal where heaven encountered earth and the impossible became possible. The natural and visible world came together with the eternal and invisible to create a co-existing reality. In years to come, the story location would be memorialized by Tanny as a chronicle of the early days of the shepherds. Its locale would be overgrown and forgotten.

"How long has it been since we left home?" asked Roee.

All agreed it had been a day and a half.

"I've been waiting to tell you about an unusual event Maria and I had.....It took us only one day to get home from the upper valley."

"That couldn't be possible," stated Dodee. "But since you got back, I'm warming up to the idea that Papa is doing greater things than I've ever seen before."

"Maria and I passed through a fracture in time and space, and what should have been a day from the valley to this spot and another day and a half from here to home was merely hours. I can't wrap my head around that feat."

Maria verified that something had taken place. Although she didn't recall the initial journey, she shared her experience forgetting Mama Shepherd couldn't understand her. Dodee heard goat chatter instead of words and broke out laughing. Catching herself, Maria and the rest joined in realizing what had happened.

"Roee," said Dodee with a smile. "Please tell Maria I'm sorry about laughing at her. I feel like the odd duck here," she continued with a chuckle. "But it's so funny."

While Roee translated Dodee's sentiments her eyes were drawn skyward to watch something curious. Her focus trailed across the skyway with a strange gaze.

Her countenance morphed from inquisitive to dread. Dodee screamed in terror and raised her arms in protection. The impact of an phantom confrontation knocked her back several feet. Unconscious, she laid on the ground in a disheveled heap.

Long minutes passed before she stirred and groaned briefly. Opening her eyes cautiously, she slowly recognized where she was and laughed at the concerned familiar faces looking back at her. She wasn't ready to talk, but motioned like she wanted help to a sitting position. Still laughing she tried to stand. But being too wobbly-legged she decided against it.

Roee sat cross-legged beside her smiling at her peculiar condition. He understood that she had experienced something and held her hand and while waiting for her wits to return. Her eyes showed resolve as her laughter toned down to a chuckle.

The Return

"I saw an eagle."

When she spoke, hearing herself sounded funny and the hilarity returned. The laughter was contagious and drew Roee into it. They fell together in a dog pile of arms and legs.

The girls looked on astonished at the ridiculous humans. However strange their actions, it was riotous entertainment. Maria turned to Carrie saying, "I love hearing them laugh."

When she said that, Dodee turned toward her and covered her mouth with both hands. Still giggling and eyes wide with glee, she got up on her knees. Taking Maria's head between her hands she lovingly and slowly declared: "I heard what you said!"

Dodee, Maria and Carrie squealed with delight.

Roee shook his head, delighted to watch another portal experience unfold.

Dodee continued giggling while her rubbery legs attempted to stand. They felt awkwardly detached, like they had minds of their own. Giddy with expectancy, she bumbled to a nearby log and sat down with unrefined clumsiness.

She made little attempt to regain her composure, and enjoyed the moment.

"Can you give me some idea about what happened?" Roee probed.

"While you were telling Maria what I said," she began, "I saw an eagle soar past a big opening in the trees. It looked.......regal and noble floating on the thermals. Then I watched it curl its wings and dive as if it spotted some kind of prey on the ground. It swooped down faster and faster, then swerved directly toward me with its talons extended. At the last second, it turned into a fireball........And that is when I screamed."

She resumed her giggling and said: "Next thing I remember, I'm waking up with all of you looking at me grim-faced. It was too hilarious. I suppose I looked as funny as you guys did at that moment."

The air was filled with "wow" and "amazing" and "oh my gosh" all at the same time. "This is beautiful," said Roee. "While you were out, what was going on?"

"When the fireball hit me I felt heat everywhere inside and out. More than anything, I experienced an intoxicating happiness. I'd like to stick that in a bottle and have a big glug of it every morning. I could face any day with that!"

The laughter started again.

"It's just like you said Dodee. Papa is a good, good father."

Roee settled back against the log Dodee was sitting on and began to hum a tune.

"You come Lord, in baptisms of fire

We yield and bow to your desire

And now we come to give you praise

Yes Lord Jesus, our hearts are raised"

"An eagle soaring is your frame

Awesome wonders come in your name

On your wings you give us flight

And with joy we love and carry light"

"Great is the glory of our King on high

Love is the gift that draws us nigh

Drinks of joy may cause to stumble

Tastes of your mercy keep us humble"

"Kindle your fire from golden bowls

Boldness and strength pour into our souls

Show us your way to the throne with praise

Your blazing home in our heart we raise"

By end of the song the forest reverberated with the words and music of his voice. The surrounding creation was responding to the praise of the creator. And the creator was responding to the praise from his creation.

During their praise, a raccoon family entered the circle, attracted by an irresistible presence that filled the atmosphere.

"Are you the family I ran into the last time I was here?" queried the shepherd.

"Yes we are," responded father raccoon nervously. "It is a terrible thing to understand the voices of humans. And unusual to run into people who are not hunting us. Are you a hunter?"

"Not for raccoons, my friend. But when I need food, I do hunt and fish."

"Well, we like fish too. And I'm glad to hear that you are not hunting us. You are humans of a different sort and we came to meet you. Our names might be difficult for you to pronounce because we use noises to call each other. So you can call us whatever you like."

"For now," responded Rohee, "may we call you friend? If we think of something else, we will call y'all by that."

"Since the first time you came through here," started father raccoon, "our neighborhood has become a safe place for all animals, even the bears. There is such strong peace, we find it easy to get along. The last time you came with miss goat here, we saw something strange. When you walked away, you left the ground and went quickly among the tree tops. We have never seen a human walk like that. How do you fly without wings?"

"I can't explain that my friend," replied Roee astonished. "I don't think I can explain anything that happens in this grove. Our creator is mysterious and beautiful and has many wonders. Why he would choose to work miracles in this remote patch of earth where few can see them can only be explained by the one who does them......Father raccoon, are there other animals who know about us?"

"Oh yes," he responded. "But they are afraid that you might hurt them. So they did not come. Because you have been so kind, we thought we could risk being seen by you. The last time, you did not stay long and we were still afraid. As for the others, if you come back this way, you may have the opportunity to speak with them. Will you be coming back?"

"Yes, my friends," interrupted Dodee. "Mama raccoon, how many little ones have you had?"

"Oh my," said mama raccoon, "I do not keep count. We have three with us now as you see. But they will leave as they are trained about life in the forest and will go off and have their own families. Then we will have more. It has been this way for many seasons. Do you have little humans?"

"Not yet little mama, but there will be soon. Could we bring them back for you to meet them?"

"Oh yes indeed," responded the mother, "I would like to meet your children."

Because raccoon hospitality is peculiar, they simply turned to leave. It is not their custom to say goodbye.

The four looked at each other and smiled. The day felt delightfully normal.

Without another word, things were gathered,

loaded and the area tidied up. The group was back on the trail until night fall.

Along the way, Roee and Dodee tried talking with deer and rabbits and birds and such. Finding their encounters met with fear and suspicion, they concluded it unwise to befriend them. When wild animals lose their fear of man they become easier prey for hunters.

Unknown to them word about them spread quickly. And not all the creatures were happy about them being there. Nara saw them as a threat to his domain.

In envy, he spread lies among the bears to gain some cronies for his cause of resistance. He felt they owed him for the free meals he left lying around.

––––––––––––––––––––––

The quartet spent the evening around a warm fire reliving highlights of their day and enjoying the emotional warmth of togetherness. The girls were overjoyed about Mama Shepherd's new gift. It opened a new realm of bonding having a mothers' heart around. Although Dodee wasn't a mother yet, she was well prepared for the role.

Maria looked forward to seeing her friends again and introducing Carrie to the flock. Carrie was eager to expand her social world. Maneuvering the ins and outs of flocking would be a welcomed education. Mama Shepherd assured them they would handle it well.

According to Papa Shepherd's estimation there is at least half a day's journey remaining to Wonder Valley.

The Return

He recommended a good night's sleep and an early start in the morning.

The new day had progressed to early afternoon when they arrived at the manzanita grove. Before going through, Roee scouted the area and listened intently to be certain they were safe. Assured, he stepped into the opening and motioned the others to follow.

"It won't be long," said Roee, "and we will be at the watering hole."

The rest got under way while the shepherd paused for another look around. Again, he noted that the area was vulnerable and needed fixing.

The water haven afforded a refreshing drink for the girls and replenishment of supply for the shepherds. Satisfied, they headed up the corridor toward the main pasture.

As they approached, an uproar ensued as the goat populace came running in their direction. The din of questions, well-wishes and introductions was heard across the valley as many chattered at the same time. Greater volume to be heard formed a noise swell. Dodee described it later as "a hoot to behold."

Dodee was unprepared for the level of curiosity. Nannies and kids pressed to ask questions and make introductions. She settled in to converse as best she could with all the chaos, asking about names and which children belonged to whom. It would sort out with time.

Carrie was overwhelmed with attention from the young goats and kids. It was more than Maria described. Nonetheless, she made her best effort.

As it goes with goats, those more committed to eating than socializing soon drifted back to grazing. The shift in interest lowered the clamor considerably.

Roee made efforts to have Dodee engage with the leaders. It wasn't an easy endeavor. She had, without trying, become the center of attention.

Evening approached. Roee and Dodee made a suitable shelter and campfire. The shepherds ate a quick meal while Dodee's new friends gathered around. Passing comments easily worked into extended dialogues.

The two were prepared for a basic stay of a few days, then a return home. During their stay, Roee wanted to make improvements that would have long-term benefits for the community.

He talked about enlarging the pond near the watering haven. It would give them a reserve resource in the event it didn't rain and allow the shepherds to raise fish for food when they came to visit.

The prospect of them being frequent visitors was warmly welcomed......more so than the pond. Of course, the goats did not understand the relevance of a pond nor did they know about fish. Roee attempted to explain these things.

Roee and Dodee announced a tour of the valley from end to end for the following day. They could spend more time with whomever wanted to come along and whoever they happened to meet along the way.

As the campfire cooled so went the conversations. And soon after all was quiet.

The next day went as planned because there was little planned.

The shepherds spent the day exploring and talking.

They arrived at the big rock where Roee had his vision and shared every detail with Dodee from his journal. The vision was enveloped in mystery. Roee had not understood about the life giving forces set in motion the day he had it.

Midway through the day, Dodee wanted to mingle with the goats then spend some time alone. Roee was certain he could find something to keep him occupied and released her to her heart's desires.

The day proved fruitful building relationships among them.

Tanny told stories by the campfire that night, holding the kids captive to every word. Roee was attentive for historical details and spiritual clues about the origins of this remote tribe of goats.

The Return

KIDNAPPED

The golden globe on the horizon insisted on penetrating the fog. The misty haze evaporated as the valley warmed, revealing the prismatic diamonds left by the morning dew in the meadow.

Well-fed goats settled by mid-morning for a respite either chewing cud or napping. Others got on with the business of the day; their innate commitment to consumption.

Carrie, Finnegan and Scampy ate till content and instead of relaxing with the others, made their way to the creek. With their thirst satisfied, they milled about chatting around random thoughts.

In their verbal wanderings, Tanny's masterful story telling came up. His brilliant knack for leaving out strategic details to stimulate the listener to ask questions and want more was pointed out. And with a keen sense for timing and detail, his hearers looked forward to story times as much as he did.

Carrie was new to Tanny's chronicles and quickly grew to relish them. Like her sister Maria, Carrie enjoyed the company and unfolding lives of others. Tanny's tales gave life a pictorial perspective.

Carrie's curiosity was stirred when she heard Tanny's account of Finnegan's birth and what it meant in light of goat tradition. Speculating what Finnegan's private thoughts might be, she looked for an opportunity to probe that sanctum when the other goats were not around to tease him into silence. This walk occasioned that potential.

Her only reluctance was influenced by Scampy's presence. His friendly teasing, if there were to be any, would be more acceptable to Finnegan than the thoughtless mockery of the others. With that understanding, she forged ahead.

"Finnegan," stated Carrie, "Tanny says in the traditions of the goats there is mysterious meaning surrounding your birth and their unusual conditions. He hasn't exactly said much about those details. What do you know about them? What do they mean to you?"

"First off, would you call me Finny? Only the older goats call me Finnegan."

"Sure, I'd love to," rejoined Carrie.

"I always call him Finny," interjected Scampy, not wanting to be left out. "He's like my brother."

"Yes, I can see you two care a lot about each other," mused Carrie. "Does that mean I can call you Scamp?"

"I don't think so," said Scampy slowly and thoughtfully. "My Mama says that scamp has a different meaning. She says it means 'mischievous rascal.' She named me Scamper because I love to run, and it was shortened to Scampy by the others. I'm not a mischievous rascal am I Finny?"

"Do you know what mischievous rascal means, Scampy?" responded Finny.

"Not really."

"There is a fun side and a mean side to mischief and rascality, Scampy. You would be all the fun parts without any mean parts. I love your humor and the practical jokes you play on us. But I would never call you Scamp........well, almost never."

"Getting back to your question, Carrie," Finny continued, "the traditionalists say I am labeled for something they call a 'special destiny.' The elder goats tell me I have a lot of responsibility to be an example to the younger kids because some day I will be their leader. They fill my head with do's and don'ts and constantly remind me how I should act and what I should think."

Unexpected frustration rose in Finny as he spoke. "Carrie, I feel like a performer. I feel like I'm being shaped into something I'm not by our traditions and the opinions and requirements of the older ones. I have my own ideas about what I want to do and the fun I want to have. I don't want to grow up to be a grumpy, unhappy old goat like Willie, making life hard for everybody around me."

"Come on Finny!" interrupted Scampy, stopping Finny's rant. "Willie isn't grumpy and hard to get along with. He's just had a lot of experience."

"It's different with you Scampy, you're a free spirit," responded Finny in defense. "Willie doesn't treat you the same way he treats the other kids. Haven't you noticed?"

"I don't believe that, Finny!" said Scampy raising his voice in the process.

"Hold on guys," pleaded Carrie, stepping in to make peace. "We can talk about this calmly. No need to butt heads."

A couple of deep breaths and sighs, and the tone moved back to calm.

Carrie asked: "Have you tried talking to the older goats about it? Willie, Tanny, Sully and the others?"

"Yeah once," sighed Finny, "They told me I was being disrespectful and unsubmissive, whatever that means. You guys are the only ones I have said anything to about it since then. I guess some of my bother leaked out. It really gets me going. I'm sorry I unloaded on you Scampy."

"I think we could talk to Roee and Dodee about it, Finny. They're wise and understanding. They're shepherds," concluded Carrie.

"I did talk to someone else about it not too long ago," confided Finny. "I met him when I was taking a walk by myself. His name is Nara and he listens to my complaints. He doesn't mind talking about my troubles and wants to be my friend. He understands my frustrations and offered to help me discover the real me. I didn't know what he meant by that. So I told him I would think about it and maybe come and find him later. He just smiled and said he would come and find me after he got back from a journey he was taking."

"What did he look like Finny?" quizzed Carrie.

"He's a light brown color and doesn't look like us. But he's about the same size as an older goat and has a pleasant sounding voice. He's very nice to me," stated Finny. "Everybody talks badly about him, but I don't believe it."

"I don't think I've ever met him, but you should be careful," cautioned Carrie. "You should never be out walking by yourself and cut off from help if you need it. Roee said that some creatures appear to be nice, but are not nice at all. He calls them coyotes, wolves and mountain lions. They like to carry goats away and eat them. And they get away with it easily if a goat wanders from the flock."

"Yeah, Tanny knows stories about how some of our tribe have simply vanished never to be seen again," said Scampy excitedly, "It happened to Finny's mama. It's spooky stuff and great for late-night story time. I think it would be fun if we could get Tanny to share some tonight."

Finny and Carrie chuckled and rolled their eyes at what Scampy said. "Yeah, yeah, we should all get rattled and scared before turning in for the night," said Finny as he and Scampy playfully butted heads.

The three friends continued walking as they talked, paying little heed to their surroundings. Their casual roving carried them to a manzanita grove.

From behind came a low voice familiar to Finny.

"Hello Finny, I see you brought some friends with you," purred Nara. "Would you like to introduce me?"

"Hi Nara," replied Finny with a smile. "We were just talking about you."

Nara returned his best sophisticated smile, keeping the three unsuspecting of his intentions.

"Yesssss," chuckled Nara, "I couldn't help but hear. No worries, I totally understand the shepherd's concerns. There's another world outside of this pleasant valley of ours. One filled with deception and danger and......other bad things you don't need to know about."

Carrie felt a foreboding about this situation. It's that feel girls get about life's events. Carrie called it intuition; a knowing beyond the brain's ability for words.

Her senses went on full alert. This animal looked familiar and her mind grew busy scanning memories. Within a moment, her eyes flared with recognition.

Without thought or concern for herself, she ran the short distance to Nara with uncommon boldness. Her head down, she butted him to the ground yelling "Run for it, guys! Go for help!"

Nara sprang to his feet, ready for a counterattack.

"I remember you, I've seen you in the village!" bellowed Carrie, distracting the big cat from going after the others.

"Sorry I overlooked you, my dear," hissed Nara disdainfully.

Scampy bolted, and was at once out of reach and heading for help.

Finnegan froze, part due to fear and the other part his confusion about suddenly perceiving Nara as a threat and enemy. By the time he got his head about him, it was too late to escape the danger.

Carrie started a second charge at Nara. But this scuffle was child's play for a seasoned fighter like Nara. He side-stepped her assault deftly and grabbed her with his claws. Surrounding her neck with his powerful jaw, he broke it instantly. Nara calmly and gently laid her limp and breathless body to the ground.

"I will be back for you," said Nara without emotion. His inference was to the meal he would make of her upon his return.

His thoughts now turned to his plans for Finny. He slowly and confidently walked up to his trembling prey and with his big left paw, knocked Finnegan to the ground.

"Snap out of it knucklehead. Unless you want to die like your friend, you're coming with me. I have friends interested in your......uhhh.......special qualities. You're about to discover the real you."

With those words echoing in Finny's terrified heart, Nara laughed deep and loud.

Scampy raced into the meadow at the inside edge

of the dogleg. Leaping over anyone in his way, he headed for the group where Roee was standing with Willie, Sully and Tanny.

Through labored gulps of air and what few words he could mutter, Scampy's hysteria ignited their attention to his urgent message.

"Help.... ahhh.....help.....Finny.....ahhhh.......Carrie."

Willie quickly bellowed, "Stop blubbering and pull yourself together! What's the problem boy?"

Tender Sully shook his head at Willie's insensitivity and pleadingly looked to Roee for support. "Is there anything you can do?" his eyes begged.

The shepherd kneeled and scooped the distraught kid in his arms. Simply holding him and letting his emotions find comfort, Roee whispered to Scampy, who had obviously experienced a disquieting shock.

The soothing demeanor of the shepherd breathed peace to Scampy's traumatized soul. Catching his breath and heart, he readied his explanation.

"We were out walking and...."

"Who is we, boy," barked Willie.

"Give him a chance, Willie," pleaded Sully.

"Sully," declared Willie urgently. "we are wasting time! We need to act on this now!"

"Finnegan, Carrie and I were out walking and

having a long talk. We wandered into the forest near the manzanita grow and ran into this big animal. Finny called him Nara"

Everyone in the group responded with: "Oh no," and "Oh my gosh" and "Poor kids."

Maria's heart sank as she cried out: "No, not Carrie, not my sister...please no."

"Carrie fought him to protect us," continued Scampy. "She managed to get off a good hit and yelled at us to run. I ran like crazy, but I think Finnegan stayed to fight too. I couldn't tell. I was too scared to think straight and running too fast to look back."

"We have to go help them," wailed Maria.

"Maria," replied Roee. "whatever is going to happen has already happened. We will go to them as soon as we can find Dodee. She needs to come with us."

Roee foresaw tragic circumstances ahead and felt having Dodee with him to mother the pain of it a necessity.

They found Dodee at the little shelter preparing a meal for the two of them.

The look on the shepherd's face and somberness of the flock told her there was a problem needing her special attention. As Roee sat down, she knew it would be unpleasant.

"Nara has paid the flock a visit," he began. "Carrie and Finnegan are missing. We need to pray....and I really need your help."

The two shepherds knelt on the ground and petitioned the Great King.

"Papa, we come to you knowing that everything works out for our good when we come in gratefulness for your kindness and mercy and power and love. We know you have the last say in all of the events in our life and where we cannot protect our flock, we ask for your intervention. Please go with us as we look for Carrie and Finnegan. And we leave the results to your most gracious will. In your great and mighty name we ask. Amen."

As the two waited for word from the Great Shepherd, Dodee seemed to look into another realm. She got up with hope in her eyes and simply stated: "We need to get going. Where are they?"

"Out by the manzanita grove where we first came in," replied Roee.

The troop took about twenty minutes to get to the manzanita thicket. But it took no time at all when they arrived to figure out Carrie had lost her battle with Nara. As Roee knelt to touch Carries lifeless body, tears of anger and sadness enveloped him.

Dodee rebuked him quickly, "Don't go by what you see and feel! Our weapons are great and life is waiting to overtake death."

Kneeling beside her husband, she looked into his

eyes.

"Papa gave me a vision."

She laid hands on Carrie and proclaimed confidently: "By the sacrifice of the Great Lamb and the word of his mouth that he has all authority and brings life to the dead, I speak life now in his great name to this precious kid. Carrie, I say to you arise and live. Arise and live."

Waiting expectantly for their prayer to be answered, they gave Papa thanks for all his goodness and kindness they had experienced in their years of friendship and service for their beloved King.

Roee detected the first signs of warmth and looked up at Dodee. Smiling, he nodded in affirmation. What she decreed was becoming reality. Carrie was breathing. Her neck cracked and popped.

Before she returned to consciousness, Carrie was heard pleading: "Oh, it is so beautiful here. Please don't make me go back."

The two shepherds supported her while she regained strength and found her footing. Moving her head about, she tested the mobility of her neck, then looked around the crowd of witnesses.

Awe was thick in the after effects of this miracle. Those who followed the shepherds had witnessed something they may not see again. A goat, dead for over an hour, was brought back to life by an expression of God's power and love. It would change the way they viewed life from this day on.

For Roee, it was a confirmation of their calling to radically transform the life flow of this valley. And yet, as the assembly burst into celebration, his enthusiasm was subdued by the sober fact that Finnegan was still missing from their numbers. His fate must be determined before his emotional momentum could move forward in a healthy way.

The shepherd encouraged everyone to head back to the meadow. Upon arrival, the energy of excitement surrounding Carrie's return was at the edge of pandemonium.

The various reports and assumptions would take determination to figure what was fact and what was fanciful opinion. But Tanny was on the job with his superior sleuthing. His findings would undoubtedly be an accurate history.

Roee seized a walking stick and set out to track Finny. By mid afternoon the warm spring sun offered a scarce few hours to aid his search.

He stopped at the manzanita grove in hope of finding a trail. With goats milling about earlier, hoof prints were everywhere. It took awhile to locate the lion tracks and begin his journey. He determined that Finny was walking with the lion, which gave his heart relief. Finny was still alive.

Nara was no dummy on the trail. He knew he

would be followed and was better acquainted with the terrain away from the valley than the shepherd. His advantage of familiarity with an old lava flow would leave his tracker without a clue about where the lion was headed. When he arrived at the lava flow with its hard ground, he changed direction to make tracking more difficult.

He was consumed with satisfaction that he would have the last laugh on the shepherd. Roee showed him no small disrespect at the manzanita grove. He was getting even by stealing this cherished goat and grinding him into slavery. In his eyes, it was fitting retaliation. And for himself, it would profit his status as an upstanding member of his community. "Honor among thieves" he said proudly to himself.

As the thought warmed his evil heart, he smiled at his catch and said: "Now remember young Finnegan. If you try to get away, I will be delighted to have you for my next meal. If you stay with me and do what I tell you, I may show mercy and allow you to live."

His next thought he kept to himself: "What you're about to experience can hardly be called living."

About two hours into tracking Finny and Nara, Roee arrived at the lava flow and his heart sank. Only another miracle would make trailing Finny possible. Looking around for more signs without success, he realized Nara had out-smarted him.

In humility he flattened his hands over his heart

and fell to his knees.

"Forgive me Papa, I lost one of the flock you gave me. What do you want me to do?"

It had been an emotional afternoon and tears of defeat streamed down his cheeks. For a moment, in the weariness of the day, Roee forgot the faithfulness and love of Papa. But Papa would not let him forget.

The shepherd had been faithful and had not been careless with Finnegan. It was Finnegan who had been careless and not guarded his heart. And now he was snared by Nara.

The good shepherd heard these words: "I know the end from the beginning. There is nothing too hard for me. I will watch over Finnegan, my son. And you will glorify me in it. You have been faithful. Be encouraged and return to your flock."

Roee received those kind words with gratefulness, experiencing again the blessing of having such a good, good Father. Papa was never polite, he always spoke the truth. What he heard was Papa's sincere heart; not meaningless talk to make him feel better.

Peace settled over him as the two friends soaked in each other's company. The day had been a hard and difficult one and there was no song in him. Yet, there remained the hours ahead for the return home. Yet, he hoped by day's end a joyful song would break through his heaviness.

Excitement and awe were strong and enthusiastic back home. Dodee happily answered questions and made explanations over and again until the flock was satisfied. They understood what happened with Carrie. Dodee appreciated what Papa had done for the flock with this remarkable miracle. Although she didn't understand the context of this valley, he had opened their hearts to believing in the one who caused it.

Because of the tender and patient heart of Dodee, the afternoon moved into evening with the goats hanging out together. No one wandered away to even so much as graze. Dodee took a walk into the meadow to allow them to eat while they talked. The warmth of companionship deepened that day between the shepherds and goats. A few younger kids started calling Dodee Mama Shepherd, a title that would grow into a lasting endearment.

For Carrie, her event was overwhelming. She didn't have words to describe what she had seen and heard while dead. Serious attempts left her frustrated. But her hope was that chats with Mama and Papa shepherd would sort these things out and give better expression to her experience. For the benefit of the others, it would be worth the wait until she could find that expression.

With evening's twilight came the arrival of Roee. He rightly assessed the mood surrounding the flock would be mixed. His return without Finnegan would not be an uplifting moment. And yet, Carrie's resurrection carried a huge positive impact.

As the shepherd approached the meadow, his inner man was peaceful and he was prepared with ready answers to anticipated questions.

Sully and Scampy met him at the crook of the dogleg.

Scampy asked the obvious question: "Did you find Finny?"

"No Scampy, I lost the trail out on a rock bed. But, I'm certain he is still alive."

"I suppose," replied Sully, "that should be considered good news."

"For us, yes," responded Roee. "For Finny, I don't know. There are evil things out in the world that gentle goats like him should never have to be a part of. In fact, there are crazy things that a shepherd should never have to deal with, like losing Finny to the likes of Nara."

"Despite that," sighed Roee, "how is it going here?"

"Whatever happened to Carrie," replied Sully, "has left all of us mystified in no small way. Mama Shepherd has been answering questions and helping us to understand. But I think we have a long way to go on this."

"Mama Shepherd?" said Roee warmly. He smiled at the thought of what had happened in his absence. And reflected that he had undershot the faithfulness of Papa for the second time this day.

"Speaking of Mama Shepherd," continued Roee, "I simply must find her and get an update on the current state of things. If you will excuse me, we'll get back together shortly."

"Yes, of course."

CARRIE'S STORY

Dodee sat cross-legged on a boulder chatting heart to heart with Carrie. Maria and a few friends were in comfortable positions listening to the dialogue between them. Tanny was up close to it all absorbing the pieces so he could fit it together later like a jigsaw puzzle.

Roee approached their gathering at the edge of the meadow. The exchange stopped and their attention turned to him. Every face was asking an unspoken question.

"I'm so sorry," began the shepherd, as he stroked each animal. "I didn't bring Finny back with me. I lost the trail at a rocky area east of here,"

"Nara's apparent plans are more sinister than a simple meal. He tricked Finny into trusting him, then took advantage of it. When we figure out how and why that happened, it will be a lesson for us to learn and grow by."

"Hear me goats. Nara is not, and never will be someone to trust......ever. No matter how friendly and sincere he appears to be, his intentions will always be to do harm."

"How are you doing, love?" he asked Dodee. "I'm guessing that your afternoon has been anything but quiet."

She responded to him tenderly. "That is very thoughtful coming from someone who's had an emotionally challenging day."

They gazed in each other's eyes and with a playful smile she continued: "Well, I answered more than a few questions today."

"Carrie is such a brave heart. I've been walking her through the experience she had. At first she wasn't happy to be back with us. And I'll let her tell you why. But she's rallied her heart to make the best of something she can't change."

"To answer your question......I'm in good spirit and mind, and so glad you're back."

"I certainly appreciate your strength," responded Roee. "My day was easy compared to yours."

Roee stood with hands in his pockets gazing at each one affectionately. He was still fighting off regret for not rescuing Finny from the clutches of Nara. The process left him feeling like he wanted to withdraw in self-pity, but he refused to go there.

After a moment of quietness, he turned his attention to Carrie.

"Carrie, I really don't know what questions to ask. I've had my mind on other things and not given thought to what you've been through. Maybe you could start with telling me why it's hard for you to come back. I'm sorry you have to repeat yourself."

"If I could describe where I've been, it would help you to understand why being back here is such a big let-down. Mama shepherd has been helping me put my experience into words. It hasn't been easy. There is so much that is different from being here. If you could come up with some questions, maybe it will help me remember."

After a few seconds of considering a good place to start, she continued.

"Heaven is perfect and everything is right; nothing is ever wrong. It is without all the ups and downs of life like we have here. There is no pain or sadness or fear or doubt. Here on earth, we experience moments of peacefulness while we live in a world of chaos and uncertainty. In heaven order and clarity is normal. I don't need to be told what is right, I just know. I don't need to be told where to go, I just know. There's no confusion."

"When I first got there, all I wanted to do was praise Jesus and Papa. I could have done that forever. I could live off that praise. It's like food. And I didn't need food. Praise became love and love became happiness and I was turning into all of those things."

"When I was there, I didn't think about what I had left behind here because I was home. I belong there. I knew I was there because of a special invitation by Papa and I was allowed into heaven. Not all goats get to go to heaven. But every living human has that opportunity because of what Jesus did to get them there."

Carrie sighed and took a breath. She had exhausted her current train of thought and searched for another.

Before she could start up again, Roee interjected a question.

"Carrie, what about these other goats? What were you told about them?"

"You will see soon, Papa Shepherd. Something special is about to happen with them. I was sent back to tell them what I saw and heard so they will be prepared. And that's all I know. Whatever it is, will change everything."

"How would you describe the area around you in heaven? What did it look like?"

"That's a huge question Papa Shepherd. Mama Shepherd and I were trying to come up with the words to describe what I saw and heard. It's not easy and it's not accurate."

Carrie started to laugh at her thoughts. "I feel like I should be able to put these pictures I have inside of me, inside you. It's the most unusual feeling. Maybe you will see them if I just think hard enough. That is so strange."

Carrie paused then continued, speaking slowly to capture the best picture she could describe.

"Everything where Jesus and the Father are is alive. He does not live in or with death or sickness. God is pure life, pure light and pure love. And you become what He is. Life is everywhere in heaven and life is in everything in heaven. Life is heaven itself. We who are here, live with death and think there is an end to everything. But in heaven life goes on and on. There is no hope, because there is no need for it."

Roee leaned forward. "Wait a minute. I need to grasp that thought."

"If faith is the essence of everything I am hoping for and the confirmation of things that I still don't see as a reality, then everything is complete and available in heaven?"

"Papa Shepherd, you have a better mind than I. I'm just a goat. All I know is, I didn't need faith because there is no need for it there."

"I think I get it Carrie. I'm sorry, please continue."

"The countryside and the atmosphere are alive. The trees, flowers, bushes, grass, mountains, hills, valleys, lakes, rivers......I really mean everything. They are alive like living beings. There are other things and creatures I don't have words for that are there."

"Heaven is huge and spacious and always growing. The world around us is very small compared to heaven. The sky, the sun, the stars and all that we can see is like a peanut compared to heaven. There is no distance there. Things can be close yet far away at the same time. If you want to go somewhere, you just think it and you're there."

"I could tell you more about colors and air and other things. But can you see why it is hard to come back? Who would want to come back to this? But Jesus told me it wasn't my time and he sent me back."

"Wow, Carrie," replied Roee coming out of his imagination to respond. "That's a lot to take in. Any pictures I could imagine would be nothing like what you experienced. In light of that, maybe, just maybe I understand in a small way what you are going through."

"More than that, Carrie, Papa loves you and will help you through this. I know you won't be here any longer than you need to be."

"I don't understand. How could my experience of heaven," asked Carrie, "be of any help to us here?"

"If heaven is our true home, Carrie, with your help, we can be more aware of that. It will change the way we live our lives on earth. Humans live passionately for the stuff here. If this is not our home, what should we be living for?"

"Okay," responded Carrie. "Goats might have similar problems. Just look at the way we treat each other over food. Goats live to eat and we fight and muscle our way to see who gets the most. Papa provides enough for everybody. There is no reason to be rude and greedy. We can live generously and without fear, knowing we will be taken care of."

"There's a good point, Carrie! How do you know there will be enough for everybody?"

"Because there is always enough in heaven, Papa Shepherd."

"Papa's kingdom and his will is to be done on earth as it is in heaven," stated Rohee. "So it is written in Papa's word. But that is not always consistent with some people and their experience.....ours included."

"What you experienced Carrie, will help us understand heaven and bring more of Papa's will and kingdom to earth. We will see things differently. We have to."

"What you've shared so far provokes my heart to ask more. But I don't want to wear you out with them. Are you up for more?"

"Papa Shepherd, I would be happy to answer more questions after a little rest."

"Yes, we could go for days," stated Roee. "But, it's getting late and I am famished. Dodee, would you happen to have a morsel for a weary traveler?"

"I might even have two morsels," she laughed. "Three if you're especially nice to me."

The goats laughed and began to wander away. Maria and Carrie stuck pretty close with the shepherds; munching nearby while Dodee and Roee spent the evening talking details and sharing their thoughts.

The beryl blue of a yet sunless morning had Roee and Dodee standing on the big stone ledge where Papa gave the open vision. Standing arm in arm, they watched clouded horizon reflect the rays still hidden from their view. The clouds were engulfed with the majestic purple and gold of royalty.

Roee was relating his account of the vision from memory.

His story provoked Dodee to reflect on a moment

Carrie's Story

from the previous day.

"Just before we left to pray for Carrie, I saw a very clear picture in my mind. A music note dropped off the cliff above us, flew over and entered Carrie's body. When it entered her, the note exploded into a radiant light that was the color of azure. I knew it was a sign that her spirit was to return to her body. And it gave me confidence to pray for her return."

"You know what I think, Roee? It may be incomplete thinking, but I think the song Papa delivered to this valley is still here and it's available to us as we have need of it. Like you were saying yesterday, on earth as it is in heaven. Heaven is either here with us or we are there with it and Papa is teaching us to tap into it. What if his kingdom, power and glory isn't so much about our ability, but understanding how to let him show up."

"You're on to something, Dodee. I saw the music staffs leave their notes here in everything from one end of the valley to the other. Like a sympathetic response, if we sing his song, the song responds and whatever is going on in heaven, goes on here. Then anything can happen. Nothing would be impossible."

"Carrie's experience may help us understand some of the nuts and bolts of it. You've said it before, it is the glory of Papa to hide things in a mystery...."

"And it is the glory of kings........and queens," finished Dodee, "to figure it out. There is so much more to this still."

That moment of revelation lingered in the atmosphere while Roee unexpectedly thought about Papa's instruction to him earlier.

"Now is the time to tell her," Papa spoke to Roee.

"There's one other thing I have been waiting to tell you. During my first trip here and just before the portal, Papa said something to me and told me to wait for the right time to tell you. Let me read it to you."

"You have been faithful, my son, to the few and small things I have given you to do. Now I will do something new with you and increase both your labors for me and your reward for watching over and guarding my purposes. Be fearless. I am sending you for a peculiar and unique purpose.....a fruitful mission."

Dodee smiled and took in the message to compare with her internal processor and measure it against her heart's willingness to act.

"Yes, we are being sent here my love," declared Dodee after a few moments. "I believe it has been niggling in a corner of my heart since you returned and told me your story about new friendships with these goats. I saw it in your eyes. And every step of the way since then has built on it. And now I am certain of it, Roee."

Again, there was silence while the weight of this new knowledge settled into an understanding of a coming change. For Dodee, it meant leaving a home and life they had built in Grindlay Village and rebuilding another one here.

There was no escaping the spiritual obvious; Papa

was doing something marvelous and she was now faced with giving herself to being a part of it.

Her thoughts drifted back to her husband and how thoughtful he had been to let the bigger picture unfold for her to see before sharing what he knew. She turned to face Roee and held him with deep appreciation.

"For the last few years, Dodee, we have been faithful to the little farm and community in Grindlay Village. We persevered when we felt being goat herders was below our social station. We humbled ourselves and accepted what we thought was something very small. But we protected the little seed Papa gave us and planted it in good spiritual soil and took care of it as if it was important to him."

"His word says if we are faithful in these little assignments, he will give us bigger assignments. And now we stand at the threshold of a new door for the Kingdom of Heaven. Papa is inviting us to step through."

"As far as I'm concerned, we have only one option," responded Dodee. "We need to say 'Yes Lord' to his purposes."

Renewing their commitment to seek the Kingdom of God above everything else and accept the new assignment Papa was handing them was verbally easy. But, they also knew from experience, there would be a cost to make room in their hearts for the upgrade.

"You will need to talk with the goats and our girls, Roee. We need to let them know we are staying. And we need to figure out what we will do with our place in the lower valley. And we need to build a new home for us here."

Roee reached over and touched her shoulder saying : "One day at a time, love. We will plan, but we must stay in the moment. Since we've been here, unusual things happen so unexpectedly. Papa will show us what to do and when to do it if we stay focused on him."

"Just let me process out loud, Roee. I know you and Papa will not lose track of my needs. And you know I need a home with some order in it and a place where I can retreat to be alone with him. If you'll let me remind you, Papa has promised us a child in the very near future."

Roee chuckled and said: "Our family will have a home. Finding the manpower to build it may take some creativity, but we will have a home."

And then he began to laugh.

"You wouldn't suppose it possible to teach goats how to build a house?"

Returning to the pasture, they found Tanny, Willy and Sully and informed them of their decision to remain in the valley. It was an announcement enthusiastically welcomed. Word of it quickly spread through the valley.

The song of life imparted in the living things around the valley during Roee's vision activated in earnest that day. Agreement was made with the song and it responded with gentle and quiet melodies. In time the song would penetrate every fiber of the fabric of Wonder Valley and increase in its warp and woof to release the life of Papa's Kingdom. Through every advance and victory the song would repeat its chorus and unfold its new verses.

Carrie caught up with Mama and Papa shepherd while they were enjoying a meal near the daffodil patch. The two had been taking grateful account of how their provisions just never ran out. Continuing to eat from what they had, there was always enough when they returned for more. Having arrived in Wonder Valley with just a few days worth, it was now several more beyond that.

Carrie was ready to give a report of how she was adjusting to her return to earth life. Working through her disappointment, she had discovered pockets of heaven remaining with her. These pockets were mining nuggets of wealth for the benefit of those who sought the treasure of Papa's world where truth is alive and dynamically powerful.

One thing still vexed Carrie. Earth no longer felt like home. Heaven was home and her soul longed to be there.

She knew every human would leave earth some-day, and either be where everything is right and alive..... where the Father and Jesus reside......or be where every-thing is dire and dark because God's presence would not be there. The time we have on earth is a meager cameo appearance compared with the unending role of eternity. The choice of location is made here.

Without knowing, Carrie's thoughts of heaven caused her to smile.

"I see you're doing better today, Carrie," Mama Shepherd said cheerfully.

"Yes, I'm doing much better, thank you.....And I feel like talking some. Is this a good time?"

"Sure. What's on your heart?"

"I think it is important to tell you what I saw about prayer."

"You saw prayer? That's an interesting idea."

"Yes, I saw prayers. They have direct access into Papa's heart. When he hears a prayer spoken or thought from the heart, he begins working on the answer right away. In fact, if you can understand what I mean, he becomes the answer."

"Can you expand a little on what you mean when you say you saw prayer?" asked Roee. "Are they visible?"

"Yes, and what I saw of them was moving faster than I could move. If I wanted to go somewhere, I just had to think it and I was there. But prayers move into the Father like shooting stars and he becomes the answer."

"Also, when we pray from the heart and do not

doubt, we don't need to ask again and again. He never forgets, ever. Even if we pray and don't understand the whole picture, he sees the bigger picture and becomes the answer for it. When we pray believing, it's done beyond anything we can ask or think."

"I think I'm getting part of it," said Roee. "I hear his word in what you're saying, too. But it's hard to picture how he becomes the answer. Any thoughts?"

"Yes. It's about his names. Papa has many names. He is called provider. He is called healer. He is called the one who sees. He is called the one who is there. He is called our protective and guiding shepherd. He is called our peace. Whatever his name, he is. And because he is, our prayers are answered because He is the I AM."

"Oh my gosh," declared Dodee. "That had some weight in it! I just felt that go through me. I don't understand how it all works, but I can see it."

"I felt the same thing, love," said Roee. "This is quite an eye opener, Carrie."

"Yeah," smiled Carrie. "I believe you will understand more than you do now. I think I've given you enough, so I'm going to find Maria and have some play and romp time."

"See ya!" she called back as she bounded away laughing. "I love you."

"We love you too, girl."

Roee and Dodee sat feeling stuffed. The spiritual

food they had eaten would take awhile to digest. But Roee was ready to put what he understood into action.

"Would you mind if I went for a walk, love?"

"Not at all," responded Dodee. "I'd like to meditate on that one for awhile, too."

Roee was up and heading for Vision Rock. Quickly becoming a favorite place for prayer, it was worth the fifteen minutes of vigorous exercise to get there.

The shepherd arrived on the ledge of the rock catching his breath and taking in the view of the valley below. It wasn't hard to grasp that this world was totally corrupted compared to heaven. Roee has a pretty average imagination. When he tried to picture heaven it always looked like the view from this rock, only perfect.

But, he hadn't come this time to see.

Before settling into his purpose for coming he took note of three eagles soaring in the warm updrafts from the valley. One or two were typical. The addition of a third was a message from Papa. He would take the time to read it in a few minutes.

A prayer had been forming in his heart since morning when he and Dodee had talked. He wanted a home for his bride and coming family as much as Dodee.

Logistically though, he couldn't possibly do it alone. He would need help from able-bodied men who could cut down and carry trees for a log house. He would need materials to make it watertight and heated in win-

Carrie's Story

ter.

And another thing. What about friends for the children to grow up with?

With the list of thoughts going through his head, he sat cross-legged on the rock, thanking Papa for the good wife he had given him. The arrival of children had been delayed for reasons unknown. In the waiting, their love had grown in strength and depth. And now he had a promise for many children. He wanted to hear more about these issues but other requests churned in the back-waters of his mind.

He quieted himself, honoring Papa with the opportunity to speak first. From this place of rest, Papa displayed the design of the house Roee was to build. One end was engineered to allow for an addition as the family and community grew. It would not require major restructuring to make the addition, but setting it up had unique tricks he had never given thought to. The picture was vivid and detailed, making it easy to draw for planning its construction.

When he opened his journal to make notes he was taken up, above the valley along with the rock ledge he was sitting on. To his left, which would be east, he could see the quilted patchwork of farm crops beyond the end of Wonder Valley. It appeared to have a township of sorts west of its center with a line drawn through it.

To the west he could see the valley where Grindlay Village existed and another row of summits beyond.

To the south their mountain range continued. He

guessed that other indentions in the range were valleys similar to this one. He knew intuitively he would find other shepherds and mountain folk if he were to venture that direction.

He stood and looked north. To his surprise, he saw a good sized city many miles off and nestled up to the eastern front of the range. Large cities meant greater resources for Roee if needed. It may be helpful knowledge for future use.

"Papa, what is the purpose of this vision?"

"Son, seek first to build my house and I will add to you what you have need of. I will call my servants, and they will come in their proper time to help you build your house and my house."

"Trust me in this. The influence of my house, because of what I am doing here, will extend beyond what you have seen today in the years ahead."

As he turned to sit after awhile the rock returned to its place.

"Papa, thank for you seeing my need and answering my deepest thoughts before I could even ask. Your goodness and mercy is beyond my ability to measure. So again, I set my heart and my will to align with your heart and your will as we work and love together for the sake of your Kingdom. As your son and friend, I will go wherever you send me."

Roee knew something had been set in motion that would be accomplished solely by the finger of God. He

Carrie's Story

came prepared to ask of God with a greater faith level than he had before, and ended up surprised to have Papa reveal that he would do something far greater. It was exciting to be a part of all that was started since the day Maria wandered here.

"You are so good and so amazing Papa."

"Thank you for your message earlier. What are you saying with the three eagles?"

"Increase, increase, increase. Be watchful for increase......it is looking for you."

"Thank you, Papa. I will do my best to be watchful and make myself available."

Roee began to hum one of his love-tunes for Papa.

Sully spotted Roee leaving the forest just below Vision Rock. The shepherd had been singing for some time and could be heard for considerable distance because of the natural acoustics in the valley. Even as he walked through the trees, nothing was lost in the mood he created with his praise. It sounded as though he wasn't singing alone.

Sully took the opportunity to see if the shepherd had time to chat and started walking toward him.

"Hi Sully," jumped in Roee. "What a marvelous afternoon, eh?"

"The days seem better and better, Papa Shepherd.

I cannot tell you the difference I feel in my heart since you decided to stay. I feel like I'm becoming what I was created to be....a goat with a shepherd. I don't feel alone. I have someone to talk to and discover things with."

"I don't yet understand where we are headed or what we are doing, but I'm happy to be a part of it. And I just want to thank you and Mama Shepherd for being here."

"You can thank Papa for our being here, Sully. It's his hand and heart that brought us."

"By the way, Sully. You say you like to discover things together? Tonight is the new moon. The stars will be easier to see and I love nights like that. Want to join me?"

"Well, maybe you hadn't noticed, Shep" said Sully playfully sarcastic. "But I'm always out here."

They had a good laugh over that, but the teasing wasn't over.

"You know Sully, you're acting more and more like a human. Maybe someday you'll grow hands and feet."

"From a goat's perspective, that's a step down. Maybe you should try growing horns and we could do a little head-butting. It'll give you a whole new perspective about life and relationships."

"Yeah," rejoined Roee. "A perspective that spins around crazily and makes my eyes cross. No thanks. I like my head in one piece. Besides, where would I put my hat if I had horns?"

"Well, I think horns would be a significant improvement over a hat any time, Shepherd."

Roee started laughing then grabbed Sully around the neck, wrestled him to the ground, then ran off whooping like a cowboy. "Catch me if you can, Sully."

Roee had the jump on Sully as far as the chase goes, but Sully had the speed. Roee made hurdles over some obstructive goats and thought Sully was blocked from following. But Sully jumped over and kept up the pursuit.

Scampy saw how the game was playing out and decided to run interference for Sully. Picking up speed off to the side, he darted strategically in front of Roee taking him down with a trip at the knees. The chase was over and everybody in the meadow was laughing heartily. Roee got up breathing hard and laughing. He ruffled Scampy behind the ears with both hands then threw his head around good-naturedly. Picking up his hat, he brushed off the dirt and put it back on.

"Good block Scamps. You just spared Sully a great humiliation and embarrassing loss of a race."

"It was defeat," retorted Sully, "or de-hoof, Shepherd."

"Sharp wit, Sully! Wow, you guys are amazing!"

From a distance, Dodee watched their clowning around take shape with amusement and affection.

THE CONVERSATION

The moon was new and a simple sliver of a smile. Night skies at this time of the lunar cycle are spectacular with starry beauty that is not ordinarily seen. Like life itself, there is a different picture when the greater light is subdued and the lesser lights are given their place. What was not seen before now stands out.

It reminds us of the fourth day of creation when the earth started its clock and the theater of time opened its curtain. Eternity would go offstage, visible only by faith and mysterious sightings until the final act. Although the main storyline is predetermined by its creative writer, it receives ad libitum revision on behalf of its free will players. But the ending never alters.

All creation awaits the last curtain call with its royal cast of sons and daughters. At that time eternity's producer and director king will be honored without limits.

Tonight, the air is filled with creation's longing for a fresh view of its majesty. It caused Sully to take these moments, rest in the pasture and reflect on the events of the day while marveling at the great Milky Way stretching out above him.

Roee sensed the mystical atmosphere. Not wanting to disturb it, he silently took a stance next to Sully.

Remaining still, they drank deeply of the enormous splendor before them and profound surrealistic presence.

Sully was first to explore the magical undercurrent. "These stars have always been here and I've never questioned their presence. But tonight, they feel like they're alive with something and it makes me wonder who they are. How did they come to be? What valley do they live in?"

"Ah, you ask large questions, Sully," said Roee quietly. "I'm a simple shepherd. And because of that, a star gazer."

"This valley, these mountains and this sky, they're the world I prefer to know. And I am content with it. But this experience.........it tells me there is a another world just beyond my reach. And tonight I feel like I can almost see it; even touch it."

"Then, could you give me a shepherd's point of view?"

The shepherd continued looking upward. There was no reason to rush the moment or fill the silence. While there is a more satisfying wellspring of wisdom to draw from, there was no purpose in drinking from the brainy well of knowledge. Roee had made this point before: "It's the difference between sipping for the savor or guzzling for the flavor." Sully understood this and waited patiently.

Roee began in a calm, fatherly way. "There is an ancient shepherd who spoke something I want to repeat. His name is Augustine. I'll take the freedom to change it some for our time and place with a little goat-speak."

"Goats wander about to wonder at the heights of mountains, at the huge waves of the sea, at the long courses of the rivers, at the vast expanse of the ocean, at the circular motions of the stars, and they pass by themselves without giving thought to who they really are."

"Nothing says everything all at the same time, Sully, but it's a good place to start.......There are more important things to wonder about than the wonders of the things around us. The most important wonder is really us. And with that understanding, there are two things worth considering. The first being the day we were born. The second is when we find out why."

"Frequently, these large and unanswerable questions about the cosmos distract us from the very essence of our destiny. But it can't be denied that these wonders are fun to explore. In fact, these amazing created things provoke us to question who created them and who we are in the larger picture of all of this."

Starting with his front knees, Sully kneeled then lowered the rest of his body to a comfortable position. As he did so, he began to chew a cud. Sully was now in thinking position.

Roee had been teaching everyone the value of a good question since he came to the valley. Using the guidelines given him, Sully wanted to make sure his question wouldn't take the conversation down distracting and unproductive rabbit trails.

But before he could properly put his more important question together, he needed to understand a couple of things.

"What's a sea? And what's an ocean?" he asked humbly.

Roee used the opportunity to sit cross-legged to the right of Sully. Turning his face to the night sky, an answer was taking form in his thoughts.

"A sea is like the sky, Sully" The shepherd began. "What we see of the sky from horizon to horizon is a small portion of its reality."

"If we were to take this entire valley and fill it with water from the creek, we would call it a lake."

"That's a lot of water, shepherd. So, a sea is about water?

"Yes, Sully. And so is an ocean. A sea is more water than you can imagine. But try to picture this, if you were to stand at one of the high places around this valley and see it filled with water and know it to be a lake, a sea would be so large that you could not see the other side."

Sully took a gulp of air as he looked at the shepherd with a face that revealed marvel. What he heard in Roee's description was vastly different than his experience of life.

"Now to take that one more step. If you could stand on only one of those high places, look in every direction and see nothing but water, that would be an ocean."

Sully stopped chewing his cud and stared out into the darkness. What the shepherd said filled Sully's imagination to overflowing; like a glass spilling over. The wonder of it was beyond imagining.

"Are you still with me, Sully?"

"I feel like my horns just melted. Are they still curled?"

The shepherd couldn't help but laugh. "Spoken as only a noble goat could say it. You have quite an imagination between those majestic horns of yours. You might have to give those ideas some consideration."

"The sky, oceans and seas are in a family of large wonders reminding us of how small we are and how big our creator is."

Roee resisted the temptation to describe stars, distant planets and expanses of solar systems; stuff beyond the ability of anyone living to comprehend precisely. From the shepherd's perspective, he could see his point had been made.

While Sully unpacked the words of the good shepherd, another question bubbled to the surface without regard to where it would take him. "If the creator is bigger than his creation, he must be........" Sully couldn't find a word that would even come close to what was turning over in his mind. "Baaaaaah, I feel so small!" was all he could manage.

"Indeed, we are very small, Sully. But we are loved by Papa in ways bigger than the sea, ocean and sky.

Which brings us back to the quote I gave you earlier. God does not want us to measure him by his size or his vast creation. He wants us to see him for his magnificent love for us. Everything he created......from the largest thing to the smallest.....points us to him. But when we see who he is, we start the journey of discovering the depths and widths of his love for all of us."

"We don't know how to respond to his greatness. If we see him as enormous, we could miss the fact he humbly portrays himself as the same size as we are so we can grasp his willingness to reach out to us. It's like three pictures in one: his greatness, his love and his gentleness."

"Sully, I love Papa because he showed me his love first. Before I knew him, he knew me. Before he created all this, he knew I would be born. And when I chose to love him, he began the process of showing me why I was born."

"Shepherd?"

"Yes, Sully."

"It's easier to see Papa's creation than it is to see how big God is and know how big his love is and understand his gentleness. I don't understand his love for humans like you do....and maybe I never will. But if what I am experiencing tonight is the presence of his love, it's a powerful love and I want to be part of it. And because he sent you here, I have the privilege of enjoying this moment."

"But, when I think about Finnegan, I get confused

and it hurts my heart that he is not with us. If our creator has all this power and love, how do you explain what happened to Finny? Why wasn't he protected?"

A bond of companionship enveloped them. The shepherd moved over and leaned his back against Sully. He put his hands behind his head, looked up and crossed one leg over the other at the knee. It was a special moment and once again they looked to the stars, a visual reminder that God can do anything.

It would take awhile for Sully to find the various compartments in his heart to sort out everything shepherd had shared tonight. And over time, there would be more to make room for. But right now Sully was at full capacity.

Roee lay quietly as if listening for a fitting response. But none came. He got on his knees and looked Sully in the face. Putting his hand on his back, he said, "I don't have an answer for that, my friend. I'm sorry. I cannot explain what I don't understand. Things happen that only God knows what to do with. They are situations beyond our ability to grasp for their wisdom and long-term purposes.

"What happened to Finny saddens me deeply. But Papa has told me that he has the problem worked out already. And I know I can trust him to follow through on his word."

Shepherd and Sully remained pensive a few moments.

"Maybe," considered Roee, "this is on your heart to

stir us to ask Papa to do something instead of us trying to figure it out. What do you think?"

"You mean prayer?" asked Sully.

"Yeah."

"With all we have talked about tonight," said Sully, "I can picture him doing just about anything."

"Nothing is impossible with God, Sully."

"What do we do? What do we say?"

"Let's just listen for a minute, then we will ask from our hearts."

"This would be a good time for a song," thought Roee. He let the words of a new song kindle in his heart. Humming, he felt the fire swell. The Spirit's presence increased as their hearts turned from prayer to worship.

With eyes open and Roee kneeling under the star-filled night, a mist formed and swirled around them. Roee sang without words of understanding while a soft iridescence ignited within the mist. With both man and goat in awe and caught up in what was happening, their engagement increased as spiritual intervention took place in an unseen realm. Without awareness of time or matter, seemingly inalterable circumstances were being amended.

At the height of their encounter Roee confidently decreed: "Finnegan come out. You and your house are free to go."

The glow in the mist faded, but the presence remained. Roee smiled peacefully, but Sully looked baffled.

"What did you mean by "you and your house" shepherd?

"I had a vision of a house. Finny and another goat were next to it. I saw them behind the bars of a prison and the gate built into the bars swung open by itself. I set Finny and the house free with my words and commanded them to come out."

"I don't understand."

"Neither do I Sully. In the unseen realm, I know Finny is free. What the house means, I couldn't say."

"Unseen realm? What's that?"

Roee started laughing, then unexpectedly vanished before he could answer.

For the second time that night, Sully was overwhelmed. This time he began to tremble.

A gentle voice spoke from the mist, "Don't be afraid, Sully."

After a few moments, Sully said to no one in particular, "What am I going to tell Mama shepherd?"

The remaining mist settled into the grass as he heard tender laughter from within it. Sully was left alone with his thoughts and feelings of amazement. He had experienced something which happens to....who? Who would have such an experience? There was no point of reference.

"She's gonna have my horns over this. Papa Shepherd disappears. I can just hear Tanny's story now: 'Goat loses shepherd to mysterious mist.' Oh bother, where's another valley when a guy needs one. Why didn't he take me with him?"

Sully relaxed and sighed deeply. "I wasn't expecting that at all."

Sully was still mumbling to himself when early morning light came. Regardless of his fearful ideas, he sought Mama shepherd to report what had happened in the night. Although she was still asleep, he called out to her.

"Mama shepherd," he said. "Mama shepherd, please wake up. I need to talk to you."

Drowsily, she responded, "Yeah, Sully, what is it?"

He replayed the night's events and the portion of the conversation about Finnegan. When he told her about the presence and Roee's disappearance, she closed her eyes to drink in what he said.

Chuckling, she opened them again. "This is Papa's doing, Sully! I don't know what is going on, but it's something extraordinary. We will pray and wait for Papa Shepherd's return."

"Are you okay?" she asked.

"I don't know, Mama Shepherd. Is this normal stuff when God is around?"

"One thing to remember, Sully, God is not normal as you would measure normal as predictable or comfortable. He is God in ways we cannot contain or control. If we live to love him, we live with the understanding of continually trusting him and constantly redefining what is normal."

"It can get complicated trying to make explanation of it," she went on. "But if we simply focus on love and devotion, we will give our best to be part of it. The science of it comes from the heart."

"Do you think Papa can use goats like me like he uses people?"

"Goats are people in this valley, Sully. Elsewhere in the world is another matter. He gives light and life to whom he pleases and to those who ask for it. If you ask, you will have it. If you sincerely desire to know him, he will reveal himself to you. What he offers is simple, but may cost you everything if you truly want to possess it."

"Since goats don't have possessions," Sully remarked, "how can it cost me something?"

"Sorry Sully, I'm speaking from another context where people work hard to have earthly goods. The Kingdom of God isn't about earthly possessions, it's about spiritual substance. Whatever keeps his children from having this substance must be taken out of the way by the one who wants them. Papa will give us the desire to want spiritual realities and the opportunity to grow in them."

"Between you and Papa Shepherd," stated Sully, "I have enough to chew on for quite awhile. I think I will take a walk."

Caught Away

It took little time for his knees to discover the difference between the softness of pasture and the hardness of asphalt and it brought him to his feet. Moments ago, he and Sully were having fun watching the stars and talking about creation. Then Roee was suddenly on his knees and laughing in the middle of a road.

He had read accounts of Papa doing this stuff, but never dreamed he would have a turn to experience it. The teleportation happened so quickly it nullified any "thrill of the ride" effect on his body or emotions. It was pretty uneventful and he laughed at himself for having thoughts of disappointment about the trip.

"All right Papa, you brought me here. What's your plan?"

He scanned the neighborhood, taking inventory of the surroundings. To his right was a raised railroad bed running parallel to the street he was standing in. Its elevation was high enough to hide what was on the other side.

Up ahead was a cross street doubling as an entrance to the train station. A sign lit by gooseneck wall lanterns on the end of the station house read Two Towns. It implied another town on the other side of the tracks.

The street's crossing had a signpost identifying the

intersection. Running parallel with the tracks was the main road named Lawless Ave. At right angle with it was a side street named Little Faith Road. The thought occurred to Roee that perhaps the street names reflected the nature of the two towns. Roee thought of reasons for Papa wanting to change this depiction and it would explain why he had been brought here.

On his left stood classic cast iron lamp posts illuminating the main road. Their age showed minor corrosion, but graffitists had turned these relics into gorgeous works of art nouveau, giving the impression of living gardens at each post.

People were mingling about even at this late hour. Couples strolled the wooden sidewalk arm in arm, quietly holding hands or engaged in lively talk.

Wooden buildings lining the street were board and batten exteriors with terra cotta roofs and covered sidewalks. The buildings kept shops and business offices fashioned in a quaint architecture rarely used in modern times.

Signage ranged from innovative to ramshackle. Creativity appeared inconsistent. But what attempts there were showed elements of genius.

Beyond the main avenue ran a paved alley serving as rear entrance for the row houses on another street. Sporadic barn lights kept the alley area dimly yet adequately lit. For what it's worth, Roee made note of large picture windows and small double-hung windows, wooden panel doors for rear entry and metal stairs for the second story flats above.

While he was taking this in, a well-dressed man wearing a cinnamon colored fedora and matching light-weight trench coat approached. The hat deliberately shaded his eyes from the street lighting to obstruct reading his intent. He smiled broadly and engaged Roee in small talk.

"Such a fine cool night, my friend," he began. "You have the appearance of a mountain man looking for a good time," he continued, making an accurate appraisal of Roee's exterior shell. "Could I interest you in some warm companionship?"

From somewhere within Roee, a loving response to this man's immoral inference rose to the surface. This area was an obvious arena for evil, but he could feel Papa's love surrounding and provoking him. In the midst of this darkness, Papa empowered him with greater light.

"Thanks for your thoughtfulness, good man," responded Roee sincerely. "I have a wonderful wife and she is a true friend that keeps me in constant company even when I'm away from her."

This host of the 'hood who lives in a world of suspicion, greed and unkindness was unexpectedly touched by the shepherd's gentle response. Through the years, he had gained acumen to measure people quickly; skills which kept him alive, out of trouble....and rich. The stranger in front of him was woven of a fabric not possessing the deceits and treacheries earmarking the society of his own devices.

As the two stood in the street looking toward the backs of the buildings in the alley, a young woman stepped into one of the picture windows, pulling the drapes behind her to secret her presence while she looked outward for help. Her plea-filled distress turned to fear-filled panic with arms waving frantically. An unseen hand yanked her violently away from her supposed refuge.

The impact of the moment on Roee tightened his throat and brought moisture in his eyes.

The man in the fedora saw Roee's reaction, his own heart long desensitized to compassion. He calmly clarified: "She is his property. Unfortunately, he does not place much value on her."

"Are you telling me she is his slave?" asked Roee.

"Buying and selling is a way of life here, friend. Men, women, children, drugs, animals....it doesn't matter. It has been this way for a very long time.....You apparently haven't seen this before." It was a statement, not a question.

"I suppose I pictured this differently," Roee said honestly. "More volitional. You know, people make choices to be here."

"I can understand why you would have that opinion. It's a broadly naive perspective. In reality, our world isn't that simple."

"The people across the tracks call this trafficking. They often talk of doing something about it but accomplish little. They create laws and carry signs, but don't really know how things work here. They don't have a clue as to how deep and wide the river of callousness runs. Many of our slaves are brought here from dysfunctional families like theirs."

"How can that happen?" asked Roee, pained by his words.

The man laughed as he said, "That's easy. Desperate people are easy prey for people like us who deceitfully exploit their desperation for our advantage."

"I still don't get it," rejoined the shepherd.

"If a starving and lonely person doesn't know how to get what they need," explained the man, "they can be duped by promises of easy success and friendly acceptance. Their desperation keeps them from seeing hidden schemes.....bait and switch, false belonging, pretend love. The list is long and by the time they figure it out, it's too late."

Roee was struggling with keeping his love alive for this guy. Yet he prevailed with thoughts of what Papa's love did to save people like this.

"Listen mister, I can see this is really bothering you. Why in the world are you here? And why would you care?"

The shepherd had to pull his heart together. He found strength to collect himself. "Those are good and fair questions. And I hope I can answer them honestly."

He extended his hand to the man with a warm smile.

"My name is Roee, and yours?"

"My name on the street is James. My friends call me Shamus. If you want, you can call me Shamus."

"Thanks, I appreciate that Shamus. There is something you can help me with. I have no idea where I am. What can you tell me about this place? Where does this train go?"

Shamus chuckled and said: "Do you have amnesia or something? How did you get here? Are you a movie writer creating a story?"

"My father dropped me off here. He has something he wants me to learn or do. And when I have learned it or done it, I will return home." Roee's words seemed totally fabricated to his ears. But after he said them, he recognized that they would easily be true.

"You're an odd duck with a very weird family, Roee," Shamus said laughing.

As Roee laughed in agreement, he stated: "I wouldn't have it any other way."

"For one thing, you'll find it easier to get your bearings when the sun comes up. But Lawless Avenue runs north and south. Although I rarely get out that way, south of town the road curves westerly and ends near the mountains. It seems you came from that direction."

"Two Towns is planted in a large valley east of

those mountains. A lot of people in Little Faith and the outskirts of Lawless are farmers. They raise crops and animals of all sorts. They live comfortably and tend to leave us alone; except if they need something, if you catch my meaning."

Roee remembered his vision of the farm community to the east of Wonder Valley with the line running through it. The railroad would be the line.

"North of here is a larger city where many of my customers come from. The main highway and railroad run north to there, then it runs east and west. This railway and Lawless Avenue are just spur lines to help the farm and food people get their stuff to market."

"The people here in Lawless are ..... well ...... let's call them industrious entrepreneurs," he said with a laugh. "If there is a profit to be made from something, we do it if it suits us. We even sell animals to the farmers that are rounded up strays from elsewhere. Or at least, that's what they tell me. Nothing gets wasted, you know."

Roee's mind mulled over this man's normal and compared it to his own. What would be grievously dehumanizing to Roee was a source of profiteering to Shamus. This was a dark level of reality, indeed.

The words came gently but firmly to his spiritual ears: "These are not out of my reach, Roee. Give attention and love them with my love."

This situation stirred Roee to look deeper for Papa's

Caught Away

love and keep his mind focused on the moment. Guarding his heart against judging this man and the people here was a struggle. It would be challenging if he had to be around them every day. He was definitely outside his comfort realm and inwardly screaming for Papa's help.

A wave of peace passed through in the form of a breeze.

"Your mention of animals, Shamus, reminds me of something I enjoy a lot. I really appreciate fresh goat milk and cheese. Is any of that around?" He was fishing for information.

Shamus screwed up his face in mock distaste. "Not exactly my cup of tea. But yeah, there is a goat farmer or two about. You'll have to go over to Little Faith to find that; it's too healthy for these louts. Perhaps in the morning I can take you over there."

"Hey, if you don't have a place to stay for the night, I can put you up. It isn't real quiet, but it's what I got. My girls stay up pretty late. And that reminds me, I need to get back there and see how everything is doing. What do you say?"

"I think that's an excellent idea, Shamus."

The walk to Shamus' brothel was a short one. And this new friend was quick to make introductions to his girls and explain that Roee was not a customer nor was he interested. Shamus explained to Roee that he treats his girls like family. He protects them and provides for them on several levels. But he had to rule firmly to keep things running.

Roee spent the next few hours as a spiritual father would spend taking in new daughters and sons. He didn't correct them for their way of life or crude talk....... externals. He would let Papa reveal the inner cries of their hearts and speak to those things. He treated them like they were valuable.

Some shared their story willingly and some not at all. For some of the girls it would be too emotionally painful to relive the traumatic journey to where they are. But Papa used the occasion to care through Roee.

With just a few hours sleep, Roee felt rested. He awoke sensing Papa's presence then listened for instructions. Each of the girls whom Roee met the previous night was on Papa's heart. He brought them all by name before the King and asked for their lives to be touched by the finger of mercy from God's loving hand. He knew from Carrie's visit to heaven that once those prayers were made, there was no shelf life on them. They would stay active until answered.

Roee also prayed extensively for Shamus. In the short time Roee had known him, he felt like a son; a son that would find a home with Papa in good time. He felt that if he treated Shamus like he belonged in the family, it wouldn't be long before he really would belong in the family.

About that time, Shamus found Roee and offered to make good on his promise to take him to Little Faith and help him find the goat goods he sought.

It was a moderate walk and Shamus wanted the exercise. It also afforded him the opportunity to open his heart a little to Roee without other ears to hear him be vulnerable. It wouldn't bode well with him if the girls discovered soft spots in his nature. These things are taken advantage of in his realm.

Shamus talked about his upbringing; it wasn't a good one. It was filled with anger, poverty, violence and neglect. When he was a young teenager, he left home to find relief and a life on the streets. The lifestyle eventually merged as home and family. In time he maneuvered his way into a position that bore some material substance. He also recognized quickly what substance he obtained had to be maintained ruthlessly.

In the last year or so, his heart had been drifting into weariness of the constant tension of protecting his turf and assets. A typical exit from this life was getting killed by the competition. Getting shot would be merciful and painless. But torture carried a stronger message on the streets. Those who rule the streets know the influence of pain.

In spite of these and other dangers, James wasn't ready to walk away from the wealth made available to him.

Roee listened carefully, striving to understand the journey that brought Shamus to where he was today.

When Shamus had revealed everything on his heart, he got quiet.

Roee stopped walking and looked Shamus in the

eye.

"You're an amazing man, Shamus. Someday you will be a father and a grandfather. I see you as a man who will know what it means to be free and to be loved. You will share your message to others with powerful miracles and spiritual demonstrations. And a day is coming when you will know what it means to be a son in the Kingdom of Heaven. Jesus didn't come to judge or condemn you, he came to save you. When you're ready to walk away from this life, call on him. He will hear you and help you."

Shamus was moved to tears by Roee's fatherly love.

"I have never met anyone like you Roee. You're like the father I never had and I won't forget you. And please don't forget me."

Roee wrapped his arms around him in a bear hug. As they hugged, he said, "We will meet again Shamus. Perhaps my father will drop me off here again.....I love you my friend." As they parted, Shamus pointed him in the direcyon of a market that sold goat products.

He approached the clerk at the front of the Mom and Pop store and nearly tripped over a cat darting across his path.

"Cat, be careful," Roee blurted, "you could get hurt doing that!"

Stunned at understanding what it heard, but not

147   Caught Away

wanting to show lost composure, the cat responded: "Every move is planned. I got your attention didn't I?"

Roee laughed. He forgot he could rustle up a conversation with this feline.

"Master of confidence are you?" stated Roee still laughing. "What is your name?"

"Noah," replied the tabby with a dialect one would expect from the royal butler. "Chief comforter for the lap of my mistress and best mouser in the store." As could be imagined, Noah, spoke with an air of haughtiness and an almost negligible nod of his head, to give his self description.

"I'm glad I didn't ask for a résumé. No doubt, your fame is widely known, Noah. It is a pleasure to make your acquaintance." Roee said with a slight bow.

As Noah sat and began to lick one paw, he retorted: "Yes, the feeling is mutual. Perhaps we could have a good back rub before you go as a show of your appreciation."

As the shepherd began another round of laughter, someone approached.

"I see you have made friends with our store mascot," injected the man quizzically. "Did I hear you talking with him?"

"Yes," chuckled Rohee. "Noah and I were making... acquaintance. It's a gift I have and I suppose it seems a little odd."

"Just a little. Can't say as I have seen that before."

"Can I help you with anything?" the man asked politely, warmly and professionally.

"Yes you could. I was told you sell goat products and thought you might know where I could find some live goats."

"Yes, my brother has some. And there are a couple other farmers in this area that have them. You interested in buying some?"

"To be honest with you," started Roee, "I lost one recently. I was hoping it might have showed up around here."

"You must seriously like your goats.....There is a man that comes around from time to time and sells what he calls strays. Personally, I think he might be a goat-napper," the man chuckled, "but we tend not to question. After all, they don't come branded like cattle."

"This one is special to me," Roee sad. "He has long hair like an Angora and is a most unusual color of blue with some gray in it."

"Long haired ones come along on occasion and blue-gray would definitely be rare. I have seen several Angoras in the last year or so. Where did you lose it?"

"As best I can determine," responded Roee, "I come from a valley west of here in the mountains. It's beyond the lava flow. We call it Wonder Valley."

"Oh my gosh, you're a long way from home. And

there's no roads that I know of from there. How did you get here?"

"I walked," Roee stated truthfully. He just couldn't bring himself to tell the man he hadn't walked more than a thousand yards since he arrived. But, it was the truth; he had walked.

The man was obviously stirred by the notion of such a committed shepherd. But stumped by the idea that he would come so far for one goat.

"Young man," he said a little flustered because he knew he didn't possess the same level of commitment. "They're just goats. Why would you make such a fuss about one goat?"

"It's what my heavenly father would do for you, if you were lost my friend," Roee said boldly.

The statement registered with the store keeper. He thought of the ninety-nine that Jesus said would be left behind so the shepherd could find the one that was lost. He opened his heart a little to talk more in depth.

"You wouldn't know this, but I've been thinking about that a lot lately," he said.

Roee's confidence grew. And he seached for encouraging words to speak to his heart.

"There are many lost sheep across the tracks in Lawless my friend. They are waiting for the love you have inside of you to be shown to them. Your unconditional love and patience will help them find the path of life God has promised for all of us. They deserve an encounter with Jesus."

"Your point is touching, even convicting," stated the man sincerely. "My brother and I have had serious discussions about it lately. Christians around here tend to be rather sleepy....us included. You know, mostly concerned about ourselves and our daily affairs. On a good day, we're concerned about each other as a church."

"But something is stirring us and we're not sure what to do with it. So, Del and I have been praying for help to get us going in the right direction. And what you're saying sounds like the thing we need to boot us out of our comfort zones and take a look at people we don't relate to. Are you a prophet?"

"I'm a son of the Great King like you and your brother. If I'm a prophet, I'm unaware of it. I simply believe with my whole heart what it says about the gospel in first Corinthians chapter two and that it is very much alive today. The good news is confirmed with the display and power of the Spirit of God. Have you heard about this?"

"Some," said the middle aged man. "But I've never seen any of it firsthand."

"Maybe we could get two things done in one motion here," stated Roee. "I need some help about my goat and you need some help about the things of God. We can talk as we go."

"As for your goat, my brother might be of help to you. He's the goat farmer and I sell his products. Let me give him a ring."

While the proprietor made the call, Roee prayed and looked around. Papa was getting ready to do something in Two Towns. It explained why he was here and why he was meeting these people. Papa would use Roee to activate the next phase of his plan.

He spotted a drinking fountain and remembered he had not had anything to eat or drink for awhile. After getting a taste, he noticed the water was unusually sweet and cold. It made Roee wonder.

When the man returned, he saw a familiar look on Roee's face.

"There's an underground river that flows directly under this property," the man said with delight. "As best as we know, it actually starts under the lava flow you talked about. Something in the ground up there gives it the sweetness you taste. So we drilled down and stuck a well pump in it. And here it is in this fountain to share with people that come in the store."

"Someday, somebody might just bottle this stuff."

A prophetic picture formed in Roee's mind of the spiritual sweetness Papa was bringing to this area. The picture was vivid and clear. A sweet river of life was already flowing but needed tapping into for those who are thirsty. When the opportunity comes, he will share that thought with him and his brother.

"My brother says he might have the goat you're looking for. He says the goat should know you if it's the right one. Let me ask my wife Annie to watch the store and I'll take you over there."

"Thank you, my friend. You are so gracious and helpful."

"I am so sorry, where are my manners? My name is Jacob and my brother's name is Del. I may have mentioned his name already."

"Mine is Roee, a pleasure to meet you."

"That's Hebrew isn't it?" said Jacob. "So fitting that it means shepherd."

"I'll get Annie and we can go."

_____

The ten minute drive to Del's farm gave Jacob and Roee time for small talk about Jacob's place and the things he grows and raises. Jacob provided the feed for Del's goats and enough extra for Jacob to grow beef for himself and Del. It is quite a collaborative effort.

They arrived to another introduction and handshakes.

"So Jake tells me," Del started, getting right to the business at hand, "that you come from the western mountains looking for your goat. How will you know if any of these are yours?"

"That's simple enough, Del. I will call him.....He knows my voice."

"Well duh, I knew that," Del said with a chuckle.

"I can call the whole flock and they'll come; especially if I have some grain. But a single goat would be something new. This will be interesting to watch......Maybe you could teach me a thing or two, Roee. I could always use a higher level of goat farming."

Del's flock numbered about sixty, almost all of them milkers. A couple of males are used for fathering babies but kept in separate areas and in strong pens. The three of them walked the hundred yards or so from the house to the pasture areas where Del kept his flocks.

"Do you mind if we get in with the flock, Del?"

"Not at all."

Del opened the gate and the trio walked around a few minutes. Roee didn't see anything obvious in front of him, so he stopped and looked about.

"Finnegan!" he yelled. It wasn't necessarily loud, just a high enough timbre to be heard. "Finnegan," he said louder.

A commotion started about seventy-five yards away.

To Del and Jacob it sounded like excited bleating, followed by pushing, shoving, butting and climbing over as Finny worked his way through the flock to get to the shepherd.

To Roee it sounded like: "Shepherd! Can it be? Out of the way! Move over! I can't believe it! I never dreamed I would hear that voice again!"

Roee started to chuckle, then threw his head back and laughed unabashedly. By the time Finny reached the shepherd, Finny was squealing and squeaking with excitement. Beside himself with happiness, he jumped into Roee's arms without thinking. The force of impact knocked Roee over and into Del, taking them both down. Everyone laughed, caught up in the emotion of the reunion.

"That is amazing," Del said laughing, "I've never had a bond like that with any of my goats. This is beautiful."

Roee stood releasing Finny but continuing to stroke and rub him behind the ears. Before he could think of a response, he heard a quiet inner voice revealing Papa's heart for Del and Jacob.

"A day is coming, Del, when you and Jacob will have this kind of bond with the souls you will bring to Jesus. The people of Lawless are hungry for what you have. Love is so simple; like being mothers and fathers. Go, spend time with them, adopt them and love them for who they are. If you make them feel like they belong in the family, it won't be long and they will belong in the family. The field of Lawless is ripe for harvest. Say "Yes Lord" to what God has been saying to you and watch as he opens the gates of heaven for you to gather them in."

The words struck deep in their hearts. What they heard was not the imagination or sentiments of a human soul. It was Father's heart for them and the lost people of Lawless.

Roee knelt to talk to Finny allowing Del and Jacob time to consider what he said.

"Shepherd!" interrupted Finny. "Shepherd!....My mama is here, Shepherd!"

"Finny, that's amazing!"

Roee stood again and called out: "Megan! Megan! It's time for you to come out and go home!"

Although Megan didn't match the boundless energy of Finny, she was nonetheless wholehearted.

"I'm coming! I'm coming!" She said, hurrying vigorously through the flock. "Okay, give a lady some space here. Let me through. Excuse me."

As she bounded the last ten feet, Finny spoke up: "Mama, this is the shepherd I was telling you about."

"Pleased to make your acquaintance, Megan."

"Charmed, I'm sure," stated Megan, trying to be funny. "Really, I am overjoyed to be going home. Thank you, thank you, thank you."

It had become obvious to Del and Jacob a conversation was taking place between shepherd and goats.

"Are you some kind of goat whisperer or something?" Del asked.

"Not only that," exclaimed Jacob, "he was chatting it up with my cat at the store. He knew Noah's name before I could tell him. Maybe you talk to all the animals?"

Not wanting to make a big deal of it, he simply stated: "Something like that, I guess. We understand each other. This one is Finnegan's mother Megan. She's been missing for a long time."

"Are there any others, Megan?"

"Yes, but they were born here and the mamas are no longer with us. They don't know another home."

"Okay," responded Roee, remembering his prayer time with Sully. "Del, these two are the only ones that make a difference to me. Are you satisfied that these are from my flock? Do I owe you anything?"

"I'm satisfied, Roee," replied Del. "And you don't owe me anything. I'll be watchful next time that vender comes through here.....What are you going to do now?"

"We start the walk home, Del."

"Please, let me give you a ride to the front side of the mountains. It will save you lots of time and energy. Speaking of energy, Kathy is making lunch for us. Can you stay and have a bite first?"

"I would enjoy that very much."

"Hey Jake, why don't you get one of the boys to watch the store so Annie can come over and join us."

"Great idea," responded Jacob.

The next two hours and a half were filled with food, discussion about the things of God and the people of Two Towns. Encouragement, love and prayer flowed freely.

Then, with goats loaded in Del's truck, they made the drive to the end of the road and the base of the mountains.

Del said goodbye and pointed Roee in the direction of the old lava flow.

"Hey Finny," asked Roee energetically. "Do you remember how long it took you to get out here?"

"Maybe two days," responded Finny. "But I was so afraid at the time, I'm not sure about the way I came."

Encouraged by the response, Roee stated: "The way will be easy and two days isn't much at all. We'll see home shortly and that's the best thing to know, isn't it?"

BACK IN THE FLOCK

Finnegan's autobiography of his imprisonment played several hours. He explored and exposed the details of his journey in reverse order back to his captivity by Nara. When his reminiscence could no longer avoid thoughts of Carrie, he grew quiet while he wrestled with his conscience. Guilt, blame and shame descended heavily and loaded his soul with regret.

With this sullen shift, it was a good time for Roee to have a heart to heart talk with Finny. He could restore Finny with forgiveness and move his heart toward healing, but loving correction would first provide the fruit of wisdom. Finny needed to understand where his carelessness started and the extent of what it cost him and those around him.

"Finny, Carrie's death wasn't the starting place of your loss of freedom. You started losing that when you became irritated, and ultimately bitter with the leaders of the flock. Your discontent with them made you desperate for a change. You saw limitations created by the traditions and rules; and perhaps you truly were limited. But, it was your attitude that played right into the treachery of Nara's false promise of a better life. Once you started down the path of frustration and self-determination, you became a target for deception."

"Finny, I know you understand what I'm saying.

But I want you to say it in your own words. Once you do that, you will never forget it."

Finny considered his words before speaking........ "Shepherd, all my life, I have heard about how special I am. I didn't like their ideas of what special meant and I wanted to be my own kind of special more than anything. Nara was the only one who listened to my dreams about it. He told me he could help me find my unique place in this world and I believed him. He convinced me I could do that without the help of the flock and its traditions, and I believed that too. I wanted what was important to me......His promises blinded me to caution for myself and I wasn't thinking about others and what could happen to them."

"It cost me my freedom and it cost Carrie her life."

Megan joined in the conversation unexpectedly.

"I am guilty too, Finny. I wanted those things for you for the very same reasons you wanted them. I'm thinking I might have put those thoughts in your mind by what I said to you before I was taken away. Nara told me he could do something wonderful for you if I would do something for him. It was all lies and believing him put me in slavery too. It robbed me of my flock and my family."

"Finny, I was so happy to see you when you showed up at the goat farm. I felt like I had been given another chance. But I knew we could never be happy there. Your best future could only have been food for humans or used the rest of your life for your hair. The thought of that was deeply saddening."

"And then Papa Shepherd showed up at the farm and everything changed."

"Shepherd, do you think the flock will take us back?"

"The flock," started Roee, "will be happy to receive and restore you both, Megan. Like you, they have changed their view of life."

"But now you need to grasp what true freedom is. Self-control and responsibility are important ingredients of freedom. Those things help to insure that other people, or goats in your case, don't get run over, neglected or put in harm's way by your quest for freedom. Selfishness will always be blind to the good of the community."

"The flock is not aware of why you went through what you did, Megan. It will be up to you to honestly share that with them and listen to their responses. Love will cover the rest."

"Speaking of love, Finny, it's time you understood how much Papa loves you. Jesus is called the lamb of God. In old times, it was required that sheep, goats and cattle be killed and burned up in fire to make up for the kinds of wrongs that we all do."

"Oh my," exclaimed Megan. "That's awful."

"But Papa our creator sent his only son to be the last lamb to die for those wrongs. Through his death, he forgives all the wrongs of everyone who believes in him so he can be a Papa and shepherd to all of them. He would tell them from that time forward of his great love through people like me, and show them mercy and compassion along with healings, signs and miracles."

"Oh my," said Megan again. "That sounds wonderful."

"Before I tell you anything more, I need to say something very important to you Finny. Do you remember the moment when Carrie died?"

Finny broke down.

"Shepherd!" bawled Finny. "I can't get it out of my mind! I hear the sound of her neck breaking in every noise of the day. A hoof kicking a rock, a stick breaking, the slightest crack of anything is a constant reminder. I saw her go down in Nara's mouth. I saw her stop breathing! She died saving me and Scampy. It was my fault she died!"

Finny sobbed in uncontrollable remorse. The impact of his wrong-doing finally breaking his heart and breaking all resistance to his need for help.

"Finny," said Roee softly. "A miracle happened later on."

When Finny heard this, his sobs slowly subsided. He looked at the shepherd, then to his mother and back to the shepherd.

"What miracle?" he asked gently.

"Carrie is alive."

"Oh my," is all Megan could say.

"She was taken through death to heaven and brought back to life after seeing Papa and Jesus. It's called a resurrection."

Finny was drowning in emotion; pain, relief, sorrow, joy and confusion all present at the same time. The good news overloaded Finny's soul.

In compassion, Roee touched Finny behind his horns and ears to rub his neck. The Great Physician used that connection to work some soul surgery. Finny's body collapsed and Papa's presence came in to heal the pain, grief and bewilderment.

"Oh my," said Megan. "What was that?"

The shepherd started laughing and reached to touch Megan. Before he could get to her, she fell down as well.

For the next hour, Roee laughed and prayed while Papa created new hearts.

———————————————

The time Megan and Finny spent on the ground was life-changing. Papa carried away every sin and sorrow. He bore every disobedience and crime. Every guilt and shame transformed to hope and a restored destiny.

Megan was the first to stir.... sort of. Her legs felt rather irregular and would not cooperate with standing.

"Oh my," she stated with awe. "It's gone! It's all gone!"

"What's gone, Megan?" queried Roee quietly.

"I must have been carrying something heavy. Whatever it was is gone. I feel light. I feel peaceful. I feel truly free. I feel like singing."

When Megan mentioned singing, Finny began mumbling words in union with a high tenor melody. With eyes closed, he managed an upright position. Then trying to stand, he looked like a gangly newborn deer.

With little energy to speak, he chuckled as he tried, which succeeded in making the situation more comical. Megan and Roee joined in the laughs of the moment.

Taking note of their condition and the time of day, Roee proposed making camp for the night. The shepherd was the first to drift away into a snooze having had little sleep the night before.

As he dreamt he saw himself as a lion taking a stand against enemies forming to devour everything around him....his land, his family, his goats, his destiny and the souls of the lost.

One enemy after another came and challenged him. He fought every one and prevailed; each challenge a struggle to the death for the fruits of his life....his sons and daughters, natural and spiritual.

As further battles engaged, fatigue increased. More and stronger enemies advanced without relief. With great resolve he prayed for more courage, as natural strength waned. With all vigor gone and battles yet to be fought, he made a desperate cry to Papa.

Another lion appeared; a titan with flowing tawny mane, running toward Roee. His countenance that of a fierce warrior, he joined the conflict. Lethal paws crushed foes and tore a multitude of fierce creatures.

His dispute with them turned to hip-hop in an elated victory dance, crushing under foot with each step. He laughed and rapped with uproarious hilarity. Prancing, spinning and back legs kicking in delight, he finished off the dregs of them.

When he was done, carnage sprawled as far as eye could see. Without any sign of exertion, the great lion sighed and said: "It is good."

He eyed Roee with admiration and walked in his direction. Although his face showed compassion, love and gentleness, Roee involuntarily shook in reverence. The mood of the lion was light-hearted and majestic, peaceful and healing. Yet, the shepherd wanted to run. Instead, he chose to bow, then fell prostrate.

As the lion stood before him, he proclaimed: "I am the Lion of the tribe of Judah. I have defeated all of my enemies and carried away every sin and sickness. I have borne in my own body all the evil inclinations and sorrows of all people everywhere who will believe in me. I alone am God, there is no other."

"Arise my faithful and brave son. Go in my strength and not your own. Rest in courage that comes from my presence. Heal the sick, raise the dead, open blind eyes. With a single word, you will cast out demons without fear. Do great battles in my name and be victorious. No enemy will prevail against you, because I will fight for you. I am the Lord of every lord and the King to every king."

When Roee opened his eyes, he was again in the appearance of a lion and had grown to the same stature as the Lion of Judah.

"Go and make followers of me."

The dream ended, awakening him.

He sat considering what the dream meant. Most of it appeared to be obvious. Papa would reveal more when Roee had opportunity to listen for the greater insight.

The moon was nearly in quarter. Feeling refreshed, he deemed it safe to continue their journey by night. With no camp to repack, they were off in short order, singing as they went.

In the distance a bright star sparkled to look like a pointer. It was small, yet Roee fixed the star as his objective and walked that direction.

Within an hour, the trio encountered the eastern edge of the old volcanic flow. Another three hours for navigating its rugged terrain, and the sky was turning pale. The sun would be at their backs shortly.

Coming off the lava bed, it was encouraging to be leaving the slow pace of rocky terrain and entering the forest. Shade would provide shelter from the warm sun that would be bearing down on them.

By mid morning, the landscape turned familiar and Roee located a path that would lead them to the eastern parts of Wonder Valley; and from there, the watering haven. The discovery lifted their spirits from the continual drudge of walking.

"I see you have managed to find my captives, shepherd man," stated a malicious and familiar voice, "Very impressive.....very impressive indeed."

The voice came from behind and to their right. That area was treed densely and shaded darkly, a well-thought hiding place for a trouble seeking predator.

He deftly bounded from his perch on a low thick limb to present himself with intent to intimidate them.

"I also see you are not armed with weapons. What an unfortunate oversight."

"These two," declared the shepherd, "are no longer your captives, Nara. The Great King has redeemed them from your devices and I am returning them to the fold."

"I don't know this Great King."

"He is Lord and King of all creation. Every creature will bow to his greatness.....even you, Nara."

"I will not bow to anyone you pathetic human. You don't seem to see the predicament I have you in. There is nothing you can do to keep me from killing all of you. You and your precious goats will not escape this time."

"Your memory is far too short Nara," said Roee with annoyance in his voice.

In a rather uneventful moment, an average sized angel with a very sharp blue-silver sword appeared between Nara and the trio. It wore a leather breastplate and although there was no wind, its long chestnut colored hair appeared to be flowing in a breeze.

The angel said nothing. It didn't need to. The picture was the message. It simply stuck the point of its sword in the ground and stood conveying the idea that Nara was forbidden to follow.

"We'll be on our way, Nara," stated Roee with confidence and a polite smile.

With all his heart Roee yelled: "Thank you, Papa!" It reverberated through the trees and out into the valley, connecting with the notes of life left behind in Roee's vision. Roee could hear the mountains and trees begin another verse in their song of life.

As they walked away, Finny excitedly asked: "Wha.....who was that?"

"Papa is always with us, Finny, he never leaves us. He is always watching our backs and keeping us safe from harm for his purposes. He has ordered his angels to guard us wherever we go."

"And his word says we will walk unharmed among lions and snakes and will kick young lions from our path. Papa calls it living in the secret place of God. It's a place of confidence where we do not have to fear. It's a benefit we get when we choose to live for him."

"Oh my," declared Megan, "that explains something. The last time I saw Nara, I was terrified. This time, I felt peace and calm. It's what I felt when you knocked me down yesterday."

"I didn't touch you, Megan. It just felt like I did."

"Oh my, shepherd. I'm still discovering all the little things that are changing inside of me because of that. It was....."

"Me too mama," interrupted Finny. "I saw things. It was like I was somewhere else for awhile, but hard to describe. I saw a hand come and touch my heart with its finger. That finger healed my heart of all the pain and confusion I was having. It was so amazing!"

"Hmmm," said Roee thoughtfully. "Maybe Carrie can help you understand what you saw, Finny. She had a similar experience when she died. But I will leave it up to her to explain all the details. I'm still sorting out the stuff she saw and heard."

"I really, really look forward to having a talk with her, Papa Shepherd. I caused her some terrible harm. But I know deep, deep inside me that I'm forgiven and she forgives me and most of all....I forgive me."

"And you know what mama?" Finny said with great excitement. "I'm so happy to have you back home. I really missed you."

With that the two butted heads playfully.

"It's good to be back together with you," responded Finny's mama, "and knowing we are going to be home with the flock again. It's been a long, long time."

The Ruction

Being left behind in the meadow when Roee disappeared almost overwhelmed Sully with perplexity and wondering about the material world around him. His dialogue with Dodee got him thinking about the cost of possessing an invisible kingdom. Both episodes provoked talks with Carrie then got him rethinking everything.

Carrie's answers to his questions prompted further searching and repeated visits to her for deeper insights. His persistence in these weighty pursuits of understanding Papa God's world brought him back to Mama Shepherd for earthly clarification.

In his quest to figure things out, Sully caught himself going in thought circles. And the cycle needed to be broken.

He found Mama Shepherd socializing with the newborns and their nannies while watching the playful antics of the kids. She was intentionally developing bonds through human touch and exposure to counteract the distance and fear of people the flock had accepted as normal.

With the group enjoying the moment, Sully considered waiting for a better time rather than interrupting them. But Mama Shepherd spotted him before he could wander off.

"Hi Sully," she said smiling. "any of these little ones belong to you?"

"Only the cute ones," said Sully with a straight face. "All the ugly ones belong to Willie."

As Sully had planned, Willy happened to be in ear-shot of Sully's friendly dig. Willy loaded a comeback and fired away.

"If that were the case, there wouldn't be any cute ones, lover boy." A round of laughter guarded the comments from being insults.

"Well, you know the old saying," rejoined Sully, "There ain't no such thing as an ugly kid."

"I can agree with that," responded Willie with unexpected warmth.

Sully looked at Willie skeptically while thinking to himself, "Willie's getting soft in his old age. He just might get likable if he keeps this up."

"Truth is, Mama Shepherd," stated Sully, "when the kids get old enough to be away from their mamas, we all become fathers and mothers. We become a big family and teach each other how to live. We find patterns of why we do what we do in our stories so it's not all that hard to know what to do."

"One really important thing is that we are rarely alone. We do it for protection. Because of it, everything is out in the open most of the time....even our thoughts.

Good or bad, we have learned how to work with it. But some of the goats have a hard time with how we do things and want to be different."

"Finnegan struggled with our old ways. He had new ideas that didn't sit well with us and it got him in trouble. We tried to keep him balanced by controlling him, creating rules and telling him how to think. I don't think it worked. It just got worse and he fell prey to Nara. I think it has happened to other goats in the past, too. For some reason, we didn't understand the atmosphere we were creating."

"But we are just goats, Mama Shepherd. And according to Tanny's history, our tribe has always done better when we've had a shepherd. What do you think Willy?"

"I've been talking with Tanny about that," replied Willie, "and watching the changes since the shepherds decided to stay with us. They're good and hopeful changes, Sully. I feel like our tribe has a better future."

"Mama Shepherd, thank you for being a part of our family."

Dodee smiled lovingly and said: "You're welcome, Willie."

Sully had come with a question and perceived the right time for asking was now.

"Mama Shepherd, I thought a lot about the talk we had a few days ago. And now I have a new question."

"What is it Sully?"

"I've compared Carrie's experience of heaven with our experience here on earth. And it seems that heaven is a much better life than the life we have here. Why does Papa make us go through this life before we can have the life that is there? What's the point?"

"I'd like to hear the answer to that myself," stated Willie. "It seems we waste a lot of time here."

"You really put a lot of thought into that question, Sully. Roee would be proud of you. And it would be best if both of us could be together to answer it. Annnd," she drew out the word to give her time to think, "if you will allow it, I would like a few minutes to think about an answer."

"Will the two of you take a walk with me down to the water haven? I could give you a couple of thoughts to consider as we walk."

Dodee gathered her canteens and they headed down the meadow toward the creek.

"First off guys, there are things in this life that we have to make choices about. You both say that goats are better off with a shepherd. What if you decided you were better off without one? Then you would have to reject us wouldn't you? And you would also have to live with the results of that decision."

Sully and Willie looked at each other, then Willie stated flatly: "That hasn't worked for us. It didn't satisfy any real purpose and quite honestly, I hated it. Why would we choose to continue with our old ways?"

Sully blinked involuntarily, he was seeing a side of Willie he hadn't seen before. Willie had become mean and grumpy from the meritless life he lived; the empty life they all had lived. The hopelessness he felt before was about himself and the tribe. But now that culture was changing. Life and love was playing a different song filled with hope in this valley and Willie was hearing its' tune. Because of it, he was changing.

"That's it Willie. You had to come to the place where you knew you needed a shepherd. We all do; I did too. Then we have to make the choice to leave the old way and embrace the new way with the Great Shepherds....Papa and his son Jesus."

"After that, there are still choices to make. And those choices are hammered out in this one question, will you learn the ways of God's love?"

They arrived at the stream and Dodee stepped in to fill her canteens from the stream's inlet. Willie and Sully sipped while their thoughts wandered.

The familiar sound of hooves at a run brought them to attention.

Finnegan yelled as he ran: "Willie, Sully, I'm home!"

He jumped on Sully's back and then Willie's, knocking Willie over. He stopped short, catching himself.

"I'm sorry Willie, I didn't mean any disrespect. I was just excited.....I thought I would never see you guys again."

The shock of seeing Finnegan alive was compelling. The effect faded and those present celebrated and welcomed Finny, butting heads and laughing. Well, except for Dodee. She doesn't butt heads, she hugs.

"Oh Finnegan," laughed Willie and smashing horns with Finny. "It's great to see you."

"Really?" questioned Finny, surprised by Willie's affection. "What happened to the old Willie I know?"

"Love happened, Finnegan," replied Dodee.

Roee and Megan casually walked out of the forest.

"Hey everybody," yelled the shepherd. "We're here too!"

Pandemonium swelled as the emotional tide grew into a tsunami.

"Megan! You're alive!" roared Willie. "We thought you were gone for good!

"Shepherd!" yelled Sully. "What happened to you? Where did you go? How did you get back?"

"The story is an amazing one, Sully, and as you can see, one that turned out good. But first I could use a hug."

Roee walked into Dodee's arms and they held each other for a long minute.

"I wish goats could do that," laughed Finny.

Dodee smiled, offered one of the canteens to Roee and said with a chuckle: "We'll have to work on that."

The valley family gathered and stories flowed as Finny, Megan and Roee told their tales.

Being unexpectedly whisked off to an unknown realm made a gripping anecdote. With a midnight arrival where local architecture glimmered of another era, the drama reached for a science fiction encounter with time travel. Roee spread his feelings, sights and new friendships before them like a three course meal with the story of their return trip providing dessert.

He talked about the conditions of humans captive as slaves and about something called trafficking and the amazing people in Little Faith starting their quest to bring them freedom.

To drive an important point home with the goats, Megan, and then Finny talked of their experiences along with the how and why of ending up captives.

Their horrors and experiences were valuable lessons and an example of Papa's unconditional love and power. Tanny was attentive to all the details for future instruction of the young ones to learn by the mistakes of others.

Additionally, they told of the healing that the shepherd helped them through on their journey home. They shared of the freedom which entered their lives because of what Papa had done for them and how sorry they were for all they had taken the flock through.

Megan related the stories of other goats from their tribe that she had run into while she was gone, mentioning familiar names. She told of their passing and their children and how their legacy of this beautiful valley had been lost to the commercial interests of greedy traffickers.

Finny got excited when sharing their encounter with Nara and the appearance of a protective angel. He bragged a little about Roee calmly walking away from danger as if it were a common thing to do.

"It should be a common thing," spoke up Carrie. "Every one of us has a personal angel, and an extra angel or two on special occasions."

"When Mama and Papa Shepherd sing, I see angels arrive in the valley to join in. I hear their music and their singing. I see them going about the valley touching the music notes that are planted here; continually renewing the vitality of the song of life the Great Shepherd brought for us to hear."

The revelation Carrie shared stimulated healthy curiosity. The others asked about their personal angels and what they looked like. Carrie was overjoyed to see their hunger for Papa's spirit realm. It is a very real existence and plays a real part in everyday life. Ignorance of it is one reason there are many in captivity to the likes of Nara.

"Papa's word says to desire spiritual gifts deeply,"

continued Carrie. "If you will ask Papa for the ability to see in the spirit realm, he will show you things and teach you what it is for and how to use it maturely."

"Carrie," asked Mama Shepherd. "How do you come to know Papa's word? Goats don't read and we haven't told you."

"When I was with Jesus and Papa in heaven," responded Carrie, "Jesus read every word to me. Well, he sort of read it to me. It was more like he thought it to me and I saw it in my mind, kind of. Although I can't read, I saw all of it at the same time like a picture and like a story.....and I just know it."

Carrie sighed in frustration.

"It is so difficult to explain these things in earthly words," she went on. "There is so much that I experienced but can't remember until someone asks a question or makes a statement that reminds me of it."

"And then, some of the way things are and happen in heaven have no.....I don't know. They're just not the same as they are here on earth."

"Anyway, whenever I need something from Papa's word, it simply comes to life. You would call it memory. But it is so much more than that. Papa's word is powerfully alive and gives life when I think it, speak it and especially believe it."

"Do you see in the spirit realm all the time Carrie?" asked Mama Shepherd.

"I'm still very new to this, Mama Shepherd. And there is a lot I don't understand. But, it seems I have some control about it. I can see when I want to look. But sometimes it is simply there. What I see is being added to. And when I ask, Papa always explains what I am seeing and what is going on."

"In everything I think and do, I do with him. Even in the fun things and the play things and the laughter things, Papa is always with me and I'm with him. I couldn't have asked for a better life."

"What you say, Carrie, inspires me to want more," said Mama Shepherd.

From the crowd came other affirming responses.

"Me too, Carrie." "I want to live like that."

Yeahs and yeses sprung up like daffodils on a spring day.

Willie took a step into the center of the conversation.

"Carrie," began Willie, "could you ask Papa to give us this gift?"

"I would love to," replied Carrie. She laughed as she explained further.

"Let me warn you now, learning to talk to Papa and use his gifts can be messy and chaotic as you learn to use them."

Sully added: "If that's the way it is, us goats should

fit right in," he began to laugh energetically at himself. The humor of it caught on with the others and they began to laugh too.

A large and translucent cylinder of azure blue light dropped slowly and fluidly from the sky, covering them all. Its walls shimmered and reflected like crystalline glass. Silver, gold and red lights orbited in and out of the cylinder bouncing off horns, noses and bodies of goats and people. Laughter and joy increased with each contact.

Person and goat transitioned from laughter to song then increased again in merriment. Raising their heads to gaze up, they all beheld a vision of a living throne with Papa sitting on it.

Jesus stood in front of the throne laughing comically and pitching clay jars filled with a cream colored liquid to the crowd. The jars shattered on each head without hurting. Liquid flowed and splattered over heads and bodies unconcerned about the influence of gravity and creating abstract designs.

As each received their unique anointing of milk and honey from their crashing jar, they sprang upward to the presence of Papa and Jesus at the throne. With the landing of the last clay vessel, the entirety of the praising family presented itself humbly in the throne room. With all the drunken joy, maybe noisily would be a more accurate description.

Papa delightedly accepted their visit and stood from his throne with an elated countenance.

The Ruction

"What I have chosen to do with you my wonderful friends is unique and will never be done again. In years to come it will be remembered as a marvel at what I can do and what it began. You noble and humble goats will be used to confound the wise and make wise the simple. I will have the last laugh and thoroughly enjoy what I will do through you."

"You will receive understanding in increasing measure, and give it away freely as love gifts to those in need." Papa paused briefly then continued affectionately, "I will send you when you become strong and willing."

"Know what I do with you and uniquely reward you with, is because of my love for humankind. You will not be like them.....made in our likeness......but you will be with me when your journey is finished. That is my promise."

Papa walked among them, laying a hand on each one, blessing and commissioning them and speaking their names affirming his love for them.

A large pasture unrolled like a scroll before them. Everything in it alive and ready to respond to Papa's word. A magnificent angel with a gold breastplate and simply sculpted sword stood in the midst of the pasture. Raising the sword with both hands, he thrust it into the thick green grass up to the hilt, causing a profound disturbance. The ruction created a thunderous epicenter as waves of creative light and spiritual shifting rippled out and down to become one with the earth.

The first waves rolled like ocean movement through

the crowd of goats and humans. It crested them up and bore them down the cylinder of blue, planting them in a heaping dog pile at the bottom. The exhilaration of what seemed like a wild ride broke into renewed round of mirth.

While the unfolding lump laughed, the blue cylinder and all its rainbow of lights gathered into a grand orb, bounced twice on the pasture and appeared to be drop kicked like a soccer ball out of the valley. Gold flakes trailed in its wind-filled flight as it sailed beyond the valley's end and to the east. It disappeared briefly over the tops of trees toward Lawless. Making an apparent bounce, the orb rose with its comet-like tail of gold and became enveloped in billowy clouds.

The atmosphere of awe did its work to enthrall and leave everyone speechless and dazed. Who would even attempt to unpack an explanation of what had just happened?

As voices found their mettle, it was agreed they would simply ask Carrie to explain things.

Their initial look-about for Carrie returned with the realization that Roee and Carrie were not among them. In the midst of this thickly peaceful mood worry had little place for consideration. Love was present like an artesian well bubbling its sweet, cool water. And an obscure, pleasant fragrance hung in the air like incense.

Cute, quizzical expressions were fun to explore as the flock adjusted to their new mystical surroundings.

Someone marveled, "I see a stream flowing out

from us. It's starting from where we are standing and goes out into the pasture."

Nobody attempted to explain it. Several actually saw it. Some could see it with their eyes closed. A few heard it bubbling and flowing. Others felt it flowing around their legs but could not see or hear it. Dodee crouched to one knee and scooped as though drinking with her hands. Everyone experienced the stream in different ways.

Roee belatedly appeared laughing pleasantly.

"Hey there everybody!" he bellowed. "Isn't that the most amazing trip you've ever been on? WooHoo!"

"Tanny, there's no way you can describe that in a story."

"I'll take that as a challenge, Shepherd. I'll find the words and a way."

"Where is Carrie?" asked Maria.

"Carrie got to stay," Roee responded enthusiastically. "Jesus told me that her work was finished here. You should have seen her Maria, Carrie was so excited. She was acting like a kid goat, prancing around and kicking up her hooves.....Maria, she was so happy. Can you understand that?"

"I think if I hadn't been there," she replied, "I would feel the loss. But now?"

She waited a moment while her emotions caught up with her heart.

"I'm happy for her Papa Shepherd. But I will miss her."

"We will too, Maria." With that said, Mama Shepherd compassionately walked to her to give her a hug.

"What will we do without her," declared Willie. "We were learning so much from her experience."

"Perhaps," reasoned Roee, "that is one reason she is to remain there. The most important ingredient of the lives of those who believe is to look to Holy Spirit for guidance and instruction, not Carrie. What Carrie gave us is enough to make us hungry for more. And Papa won't disappoint us if we ask him for more. He is such a good Father and his love for us is greater than we can possibly imagine."

"Carrie said something about Papa's word," continued Willie. "She said Jesus read it to her....or something like that....and she remembered the whole thing. Do you think he would do that for us?"

"Great question Willie. I know he would enjoy doing that for all of you. You goats have the most incredible memory. Look at Tanny and all the stories he's stuffed in his heart. You guys can do the same thing."

"I have an idea," injected Dodee. "Papa Shepherd and I can read it to you. We can do a little every day. You can repeat it to each other, hear it and speak it. As it has been said before, Papa's word is powerfully alive when it is thought, spoken and believed."

"What a wonderful idea," squealed Rosie. "Then we

can be powerful, too!"

"That's quite a revelation, Rosie," rejoined Mama Shepherd. "Jesus wants to make us powerful and loving. He wants us to do the things he did when he was here and have an impact on the world around us."

"Well what did he do?" asked Tanny. "And what kind of impact are you talking about? How do we find out about all this?"

"Tanny, you're the master inquisitor," responded Roee. "Great questions."

"The true stories about him are in Papa's word. And I couldn't think of a better time than now to get started. Mama Shepherd and I will read to you. Then all of you will hear about the stuff Jesus did. Do I hear an 'amen'?"

Everybody stood listening, trying to hear what Roee was listening for.

Scampy was the first to speak up.

"I don't hear anything. What does an amen sound like?"

Roee and Dodee burst into riotous laughter, recognizing the Christianeze that stumbled from Roee's lips. Dodee punched Roee in the arm playfully.

"Well explain what an amen sounds like, brotha!"

"I'm sorry guys," the shepherd said while trying to stop his laughter. "among our human tribes there is a thing called 'church' and 'preaching' and 'fellowship.'

Things that will need explanation at some time, but not right now. And we use certain words within the context of that culture that are not always understood by those who don't do them. Like the practice of 'amen.'"

"At the risk of boring some of you, the word 'amen' comes from the Hebrew language and has two meanings and two ways of saying it. Amen is a declaration or an agreement that something is confidently true. The other is 'omein.' It is the condition of something."

Roee bent over and picked up a large rock.

"The condition of this rock is hardness. The rock is very hard. That is its condition."

"'Omein' refers to the condition of faithfulness, dependability and loyalty. I can say with confidence that it is true that you guys are hairy and have horns. What I say about you is a true, faithful and dependable statement; you can trust it. So to agree with me that you are hairy and have horns, you would respond by saying 'amen.'.....If you understand that goat college explanation, raise your hoof."

Dodee was holding her head and shaking it at the same time.

"That deserves another punch in the arm," she said.

And from the crowd of newly enlightened goats came a unified 'amen.'

Roee looked at Dodee with a playful smile and said, "Really, I think they got it."

Chortles, chuckles and giggles spread through the flock.

While Roee walked off to get his bible, the conversation turned to Carrie and their collective experience.

By the time Roee returned, the group was engaged in a discussion about their trip to the throne of God. With more questions than answers, Papa Shepherd focused his reading to scriptures about heaven and spiritual beings instead of Jesus.

"It will take awhile for us to sort through all that we experienced," stated Roee. "As we learn Papa's word we will certainly understand more in time."

Spiritual hunger was kindled and would continue to burn strong as all looked forward to more time the following day.

Roee and Dodee grabbed an energy snack of grain and honey. Their walk through the pasture on the way to Vision Rock had purpose to meet with Papa and converse about a venture to Grindlay Village and the start of their moving process. Although a curious batch of kids followed, they kept the conversation focused on their agenda.

"With all the random events, it's difficult to make plans," Dodee mused. "But we need to get some things worked out. How are we going to get back to the house and move everything up here? Where would we put our stuff even if we got it here? Have you given it any thought?"

"Yeah, I have," responded Roee. "It seems we need to build a house first. Or maybe a large tent would work. If we brought everything up here now, the raw elements would cause problems."

Dodee giggled, "You mean like the kids would eat it or something?"

"Yeah," Roee laughed. "And the sun and moisture would ruin it."

"Speaking of kids," Dodee ventured further. "How are we going to get some privacy so we can work on that?"

"That's a very good question," rejoined Roee with a smile. "Life is a bit rustic, isn't it?....But it seems that the pioneers overcame those obstacles and had children."

"Ha!" Dodee exclaimed as she grabbed his arm and pulled him closer. "That's the misleading substance of movies, Love!.....Nope, I'm not a pioneer after that fashion! I want something comfortable and private."

As they headed into the forest trail toward the rock, their conversation turned to the event of Roee's adventure in Lawless. He explained in detail his encounters and conversations. And by the end of that they were at the overlook.

"You know, Dodee, I don't have any solid ideas about what to do next. Papa has provided so much to make life work for the moment. Our food is being constantly restored. We have almost as much now as when we started. Unless he gives us a directive, let's just praise Papa for what he's done and leave what needs to be done in his hands."

Papa's presence drew near to them, which brought their attention to singing in worship and praise for him. There was a brief and humorous hope they would simply enjoy the time without being carried away to some distant planet. With growing confidence they felt it wouldn't matter anyway.

As song overtook them harmonies blended beautifully and created a canopy of praise over the valley to echo off the other side and return. The echo reverberated again and again off the mountains behind them. With the delay effect the song sounded like it was sung by a choir.

In the valley, the tribe enjoyed the stereo concert unknowingly put on by the shepherds. Animals joined in slowly. With growing enthusiasm, the richness built to a crescendo.

The song of life Papa planted in the valley could not resist the praise and connected its instruments and voices. The trees and hills sang with baritone brilliance. Daffodils swayed without wind in slow-moving rhythm and chimed like small bells. Grasses added alto harmonies while clouds mixed their special voice of living and pure color.

The forest creatures wandered out to join in the song. Deer and squirrel, rabbit and skunk, mouse and fox, a pair of badgers; all came in response to the beckoning symphony.

Seven hawks flew in from the west riding thermals and wing-danced with swirls, dives and loops in praise of their creator.

The inspired offering was majestic and Papa received it with delight.

BACK IN LAWLESS

The development of a healthy understanding of love is likened to the care of a well-tended garden. Cultivation, watering and calculated nutrients make good soil where life flourishes. Intentionality, knowledge of its internal and external needs and selflessness are the substance for well nurtured seeds to become thriving plants, or in this case, open and trusting hearts. The people of Little Faith honestly recognized the heart condition of their community and were determined to raise the bar and make it a better place where redemptive and fruitful life could happen.

Shortly after Roee's return to Wonder Valley, the seeds he sowed in the people he met germinated with a purposeful rooting to change the broken culture of Lawless. While they prayed for design, Father enlarged them into becoming the answer. Their love for the people of Lawless emerged and grew into maturity.

Love was there mind you, and always had been. But it needed strength to overcome the storms of self-consciousness, concern of what others might think and the personal jeopardy to comfort zones and personal resources. As Papa shined a brighter light on them through encounters with himself and the people of Lawless, he would expose the quality and limitations of their light. Capturing the essence of God's heart for the searching people of Lawless and saving them at any price was a picture that would enlarge and clarify shortly. It would also enlarge and clarify their design and destiny.

Jacob had it in his heart to go into Lawless and look for Shamus. But the idea of making his first venture into the neighborhood was a little unnerving. In reality, it was a lot unnerving. Shifting into another culture was a paradigm shift into an unfamiliar type of garden. And this wasn't the kind of thing one could rehearse; he would have to jump in and learn.

But faith and love was spelled r-i-s-k in his understanding. And risking one's life and time for hopeful possibilities was vastly different than doing the same for assured results. He was willing to risk that he had enough of the authentic stuff to encounter what would probably include conflict to some measure.

Jacob and a younger friend Rigo, ventured there one evening. Rigo was bold, funny, loved people and loved Jesus. He made it look easy to connect with people in different walks of life and inspired Jacob to open up and be genuine.

Arriving in Lawless their first evening, Rigo's charisma worked its example on Jacob. He was ready to love his way through whatever encounter he would face.

With sunset behind them, assorted automobiles drove by slowly. Women with skimpy and seductive attire clustered about displaying their wares for potential customers. The culture of this environment and the dark influences seeking to enforce its turf pressed against the two men's resolve. As they prayed and walked, the grace to impart life-giving love switched on its power.

One of the roving pimps approached them, his face expressing suspicion and protection. Jacob and Rigo lacked the hard or guilty look of other men who frequented this avenue. So he confronted them.

"You two gentle souls look out of place here," the man said rather flatly. "Is there something I could interest you in? I'm certainly not short of entertainment if that's what you're looking for."

Rigo jumped in without hesitation: "We came here to pray for people, my friend. We're looking for people who are hurt or sick or who simply need a friend."

"Look guys," rejoined the man, "if you're here to do your hit-and-run witnessing crap, you can stuff it and leave. And don't drop off any tracts on your way out."

The man's attitude rolled off Jacob and Rigo without deterrence.

"Not at all, friend," responded Jacob. "We come here to love people the way Jesus loves them. No judging or telling anyone they're going to hell. It's simple, we want to see Jesus heal what hurts and reveal his kindness."

Jacob's reply reminded the man of someone he met recently; someone whose life was not empty words, but made of reliable substance. He was not yet convinced, so he tested them.

"You guys don't have any idea what you're getting

into. Pain runs deep here. Hurting others and getting hurt is a way of life. Sickness isn't simply physical, it's part of the machinery that makes this establishment operate. It's on both sides of the cash register and people like me take advantage of it for profit."

"You won't come here a couple times, pray for a few folk and change this place. It ain't gonna happen! You're a long way from your safe and comfortable religious lifestyle. As far as you guys are concerned, you'll see how ugly life gets here on a regular basis. I don't think you'll have the stomach for it.....But hey! Jump in and see what happens. Just remember, I'll be watching. If you're not the real deal, I'll run you off."

"I have no problem with that," said Rigo without vacillation.

"By the way, my name is Rigo," he said with hand extended. "And this is my friend Jacob."

"James. Make yourself at home, gentlemen.....If you can."

James casually turned and walked away.

A few weeks into their adventure in love, Jacob and Rigo pulled James aside at the start of an evening. By this time, the two were better adjusted to street life and decently free about engaging with people.

"Hi James," said Jacob ardently, "How is your day going?"

"About like any other day," responded James with a smile. "You ready to come over and join my side? You seem to get along with the girls better than I do.....Quite honestly, if I treated my girls like you and your wives do, I'd be out of business."

Ignoring James' question, Jacob forged ahead.

"You were right about us, James."

"Really? How's that?"

"It hasn't been easy getting a first-hand revelation of your world. I have to admit it would've been easier to give up, or blow up the neighborhood and rebuild."

"I knew you guys wouldn't be quitters," James responded. "You remind me of a man I met not long ago right here on this street. He said his father dropped him off to learn some things. I guess he learned them, and maybe you guys are too."

"Are you talking about Roee?"

"You know him?" It was more of a statement than a question.

"Yes," replied Jacob. "He came looking for a goat he had lost."

"Interesting, he didn't mention the lost goat," rejoined James. "But that would explain his wanting to know where he could find some goat cheese.....Do you stay in touch with him?"

"No we don't. He and his wife live a pretty rustic

lifestyle in a remote valley west of here. No phone, no electricity, no roads back to his place. I don't see how he does it alone. He also mentioned he's building a cabin."

Jacob looked at Rigo and said, "Hey, maybe we should pull our resources together and help him out. It shouldn't be too hard to find him."

"You would do that for him?" asked James, both touched and intrigued by the idea.

"If you decide to go, I'd like to go with you." added James, "I have a Jeep and some camping gear we could use."

"I wouldn't have pictured you for the outdoor type," Rigo stated with a laugh.

"Even heartless pimps like me have to get alone every now and then and do some fishing."

"I think you're on to something, Jacob," said Rigo. "I have a good feeling about it. How much advance notice you need, James?"

"Just a couple of days.....Uhh, make that three days. I'll need extra gas cans and some time to pull stuff together."

"I have plenty of gas and cans at the farm," responded Jacob. "Don't worry about that part of it."

"Fine," responded James, "let me know what you decide."

"I need to get to work gentlemen. And so do you.

Have a good evening."

A get together the next morning centered its agenda around their efforts in Lawless. Del and Kathy, Jacob and Annie and Rigo with his wife, Maria focused the subject to Roee and James. Their cheerful conversation led to a decision to find the wilderness shepherd and be practical hands to help in what was going on there.

They made plans to leave in four days and a list of things to do. Prepare the proper vehicles, pull equipment and materials together for building a log home in the backwoods and get James in the loop. Jacob, James, Rigo and Maria, would make the trip and stay as long as needed. Del, Kathy and Annie with her sons would remain to manage chores on the three farms and run the store.

The caravan of three vehicles set their sights west toward the mountains and the adventurism of an unknown destination. Two four-wheel drive pickups and a jeep. Each was loaded with tools, some building supplies, chain saws, generators, plenty of food and extra cans of gasoline.

Coming to the end of paved civilization, the next phase became the dirt paths of wilderness where pioneers, hunters and hikers had been making trails for generations. Within a couple hours, they encountered the lava flow Roee had mentioned. With no roads from this point, progress would slow considerably over the rocky terrain.

Following their compass, they headed as due west as obstructions permitted. Large rocks forced them northward slightly. Traversing the lava flow, lush and peaceful forest lay ahead. First analysis suggested an absence of openings through the trees sizeable enough for vehicles. They took the opportunity to stop, stretch legs and look about.

"Hey, look over there," said Maria pointing. "Someone is coming out of the trees."

"Good eyes, Maria," responded Rigo. "With all the camo, he's hard to see."

"It's a girl thing, Rigo," laughed Maria. "We have better vision."

They all walked his direction as he approached their vehicles.

He had a bow on his back, a quiver of hunting arrows and hiked with a shepherd's staff. His appearance was average and typical of those who spend their days outdoors, he sported a beard.

"Good morning," said the man cheerily.

The others responded with warm greetings and Rigo stepped forward.

"How's hunting today?"

"I found what I was looking for," stated the man optimistically. "But you look like you might be having difficulty with that one. Maybe I can be of some help to you?"

"We are looking for a man we believe lives around this area. He goes by the name of Roee," responded James. "Would you happen to know him?"

He looked at James with a comfortable and relaxed expression; like he had known James all his life. "Yes, I know the man very well. He is a friend of mine."

"You're not too far off for finding him." Using his hand to show direction he further said: "Go north along these rocks. The lava flow dips below the surface and keeps the forest from getting any closer than it is. There's a natural path along here for another mile or so. Before you get to the end, you will find an opening in the forest wide enough and long enough to get you to his valley."

He laughed light-heartedly and said: "It's almost like it was made just for you."

"Enjoy your time with him. He's a wonderful host....for a mountain man." When he said that, he laughed even hardier. "And please tell him I send my love."

"And who should I say gives him such fond greetings?" asked Rigo.

"He and I share the same name. And we are both shepherds."

He stepped up to each person, taking their right hand with his, he blessed each one while putting his left hand on their shoulder.

When he came to James, he shook his hand using both of his. He looked again in his eyes and said: "I am looking forward to meeting you again my friend."

James was moved by the love this man possessed and could not find an appropriate response.

The others thanked him for his help and climbed into their vehicles.

As they drove off, the man stood watching, smiling and humming while leaning on his shepherds staff. After several minutes, he turned and walked back into the forest.

"What a beautiful day this is becoming," he said to whomever was listening.

Locating the gap in the forest wasn't difficult. It was just as the stranger said. West from there and into the woodlands was a rambling natural passageway of tall grass, wildflowers and short brush. Because of its meandering, visibility was limited and determining distance was uncertain.

After some miles, the trio of vehicles came to a stream cutting diagonally across the unused avenue. To their right ran a waterfall about five feet high. Although it didn't catch the attention of their outdoor inexperience, there was no moss on the rocks that created it. They took another opportunity to shut off their engines, got out and drank in its calming effect.

"That's beautiful," stated Maria with her eyes closed. "It sounds like soothing music to my soul."

"I don't hear music," responded James quietly. "But it sure is peaceful."

As Rigo admired the green panorama, his eye caught movement behind them. It disappeared too quickly to identify with certainty. Although alerted, he made the decision to not bring an alarm to the others.

"We should probably keep moving," was all he said. "We don't know how far we need to go while there is daylight."

Engines started and the procession moved across the stream toward a curve in the scene ahead. The stream they forded took a right turn at the left edge of the trail and flowed alongside the trail for another two hundred yards. The untamed road took a sharp turn to the north while the stream continued west and into the thickening forest.

As they made the turn, the sight of a goat herd with Roee and Dodee at the front welcomed them to the end of the trail.

Behind them sat two additional men on 4 wheel ATVs.

Roee was smiling broadly while Dodee had a rather pleased look on her face.

The appearance of other humans in Wonder Valley

was rare. The convergence of humans in or on vehicles of any kind and appearing from two different directions at the same time was monumental.

Adding to the heightened atmosphere, a mild shifting type earthquake had occurred the day before. Something the valley had no memory of.

Sounds of distant engines had drifted in through echoes off the mountains beginning mid-morning. Faintly at first and increasing, their anticipated arrival in the normally quiet environment gave cause for unfolding questions about who could be coming.

"Shamus, Jacob," hollered Roee, overjoyed to capture what was happening. "Meet Nate and Isaac. They arrived just moments ago from the lower valley. This is amazing that you all would be here at the same time!"

As introductions began among the humans, the goats talked among themselves. Their noise level increased rapidly to such a pitch that Roee had to intervene to find out what the stir was about. It was obvious a major fuss was abuzz.

In sorting through the excitement, it was determined that the goats could understand what the other humans were saying. In their astonishment, they got excited and started talking. Through that process, the humans also found out they could understand the goats.

The rest of the afternoon was occupied with the new arrivals telling their stories about how they came to be there and settling in for a stay.

Nate and Isaac came out of concern for Roee and Dodee. The shepherds were only to be gone for about a week. When several weeks passed without their return, Nate and Isaac decided to see if there was a problem.

After picking up the original trail, they came as far as the location of the portal. There, the forest was too dense for their motorcycles to pass. A man who appeared to be out bow hunting offered his assistance. Acquainted with Roee and knowing where he could be found, he had them back-track to a clearing wide enough for their ATVs. He said it would take them where they needed to go.

"What did this hunter look like?" asked Jacob curiously.

Their description of the man, his clothes and his personality resembled the man of their own encounter.

After talking with Roee and Dodee about their plans to remain, Nate and Isaac felt they could be of better help by returning to the shepherds' house in Grindlay Village and bringing back as much as they could carry. With Dodee's aid, they had a list of priority items that would get life in Wonder Valley situated well.

The two men would go back in the morning and return the following afternoon.

So, what happened with the goats? Roee determined their encounter in heaven imparted a gift to the entire flock. All were now endowed with the ability to communicate with humans. The implication of its purpose was beyond Roee's grasp, and the flock was in a ruffled state.

As can be imagined, they were stumped about what to do with their new ability. Having a shepherd they could understand and who could understand them was different than having to learn how to be social in a wider framework. The shepherds quietly assured them they would learn this skill-set in quick time.

The evening was humorously entertaining to watch as six humans adjusted to the presence of a flock of talking goats. As they all sat around a campfire, Roee processed the events of the day.

"You guys came out here from Two Cities to help us build a home. You risked getting lost, running into unfriendly wildlife and breaking down. Just so you could find us and help us build a home.......You guys are amazing."

"And Maria, thank you for being so brave! This wilderness stuff is not an easy world for most women. But I know Dodee is thrilled to have another woman around to talk to."

"Nate, Isaac, thanks for being concerned for us. We had no idea events would happen the way they did. You guys need to hear at least the highlights of the incredible adventure Dodee and I have been on."

For the next hour or so, Roee began with Maria's

mysterious disappearance and chronicled most of the events of their journey up to the present.

"You mean," started Shamus, "that your arrival in Lawless was only a moment after you did a vanishing act from the pasture while talking to Sully?"

"You have no idea," stated Sully, "how strange it was to watch him disappear. I was speechless."

"Sully," rejoined Shamus smiling, "it's hard for me to picture you talking let alone being speechless. I would never have considered Roee's experience being anything more than a tall tale if I weren't sitting here with a flock of talking goats that have had an encounter with God. It makes my head spin."

"I've had the same thoughts about humans," responded Sully with a laugh. "It wasn't very long ago that Papa Shepherd showed up looking for a stray goat. His gift of talking with us shocked everyone into a new normal. He even taught us how to listen for an amen."

The inside joke was lost on the new-comers, but everyone else got a laugh out of it.

"If I may be a little curious, Roee" began Shamus. "What was your life like before you came here?"

"My life prior to Grindlay Village may be a story for another time. That man no longer exists; and I am thankful for that. But I can tell you about Grindlay easy enough."

"It was mostly uneventful and simple. Really quite

ordinary if there is a picture definition for that word. I suppose that is one of those "relative to what?" kind of things."

"Dodee and I built a quiet lifestyle when we got there. We both love being outdoors and living in the country, enjoy raising our own food and being a blessing to our neighbors. We felt it was what Papa created us to be."

Roee started to laugh. "All of that changed in one day, Shamus. Through events and circumstances I've already shared, we became celebrities in the goat community. It's been a wild ride to fame, stardom and now this great log mansion is being raised before our eyes."

"Who knows, Shamus. Perhaps we will have to build walls and security gates to keep our fans from over-running us for autographs. I can picture a custom made limo for the goats and luxury barns with the latest and greatest goat technologies. We may even need to change the name of this valley to "Billywood."

"Ha! I can just picture it now. A machine on the wall of the barn that cleans and polishes goat horns. All they have to do is stick their head in and out comes shiny, silver tipped works of art. We might even have a corner salon where we hire servants to do 'hoofacures.' Can't you just see these guys with well-oiled coats, parted on the side, that look like they're just out of the Roaring Twenties? The possibilities are endless!"

The gang was rolling with the fun of the moment.

Through his own laughter, Shamus responded:

"Roee, where do you get your imagination? You're hilarious!"

"Come on, tell me about all this supernatural stuff. Tell me what you were like before you knew God. You and Dodee are so loving, and your lives are so uncomplicated. I feel like I've known you all my life. Help me understand. What's your history?"

Roee recognized the door into Shamus' soul that had just opened; laughter and belonging had a way of doing that. He took a moment to ask for Papa's help.

"We are who we are because we don't have a history, Shamus. Papa is merciful and gracious. His word says his mercy is made new every morning. What negative history we've created is carried away by the sacrifice of Jesus on the cross. Jesus didn't come to judge us or punish us because of our history, he came to save us from our history and give us a future."

"In simple terms, it means he took upon himself your history and forgave it. He is no longer concerned about your history. He's concerned about your destiny."

"Out of that relationship, freedom is birthed to overcome the pain, wrong choices and circumstances that caused you to have a history. You become a new man that starts to be like Jesus and do the things he did when he was here. That supernatural stuff Jesus did when he was here, is now being done through us who believe in him."

Shamus, by reason of his life's choices, had become

a person who was not easily convinced. The years of hardening his heart to the dreams and desires of others for his own gain left him with an inability to feel. But since he had come to know Roee, Jacob and Rigo, the evidence of authentic love was breaking through the stone he called his heart. The reality of what he saw around him was unavoidable and implored a response.

"I would like to meet the Jesus you're talking about," sighed Shamus.

"You did, Shamus. All six of you did," responded Roee.

Shamus remembered the bow hunter they encountered on the way to the valley and the love that was in him.

"I have been looking forward to this moment, Shamus," spoke a cheery voice from outside the campfire light.

The man in camouflage walked into the circle and stood before Shamus holding out his arms and hands imploringly.

"Give me your history Shamus, and I'll give you more life than you will know what to do with. I'll be the Dad you never had and teach you the ways of my Father. Have you ever had an offer like that?"

Shamus looked at the man's hands and saw the scars of the nails from the cross. He looked into his eyes and saw love looking back at him. There was no more resistance left and he stood into Jesus' waiting arms.

Years of a life of darkness yielded before love's precious light. A lifetime of fatherless wandering found the path into a true Father's heart. A heart hardened by sin discovered tenderness.

As Jesus stood holding Shamus, letting his heart receive new life, he looked toward Nate.

"Nate," he said. "Wouldn't this be a good time to come and join us in a group hug? I know you're ready to believe."

"How can I not believe? I've never seen love like this before."

Shamus looked over to Nate with tears and a smile as big as a new heart could give and spread one arm to make room for him. The three embraced as Nate entered Papa's Kingdom.

The remaining members of the human group rose from their sitting and reclining by the campfire and joined the baptism of love.

"Gosh'" said Scampy. "We're gonna have to figure out a way to do that."

As the group enjoyed the magic of the moment, Jesus became a mist and entered into Shamus and Nate.

CONSTRUCTION BEGINS

The physical space between Nara and Ennui was enough political distance between lion and bear to keep the balance of alliance and distrust.

"The way those goats and humans carry on their affections is disgusting, Ennui."

"You're being weak and petty, Nara. Why should that be a concern of yours?" The bear's deep voice was critically aloof. "Are you losing your reputation as top cat in these woods because of it?"

"They're of no use to my plans if they love each other. They can't be conquered if they can't be divided."

"It seems that we bears ate better before you got this crazy scheme to trick goats into running off with you. Why should I care about your plans?"

Nara smiled politely at what he thought was the bear's ignorance and short-sightedness. "Yes, the sweet life of simplicity. I have forgotten when that was important."

"But what I offer you, Ennui, is an opportunity to remedy that problem. I could provide more feasts for you if you could provide some rumors and accusations for me. It's always worked in the past, and you do such a fine job of it."

"Talk is easy, Nara. And you aren't real good at coming through with your end of things. Show me the bodies, then we'll talk about a plan."

Nate nudged Isaac. "Time to get up, buddy."

Isaac's eyes opened slowly, then looked at the one who disturbed his sleep.

"What's with you being up before me?....That's never happened before."

"Last night never happened before."

Isaac yawned then shuddered at the cool air rushing into his unzipped sleeping bag. "Yeah, that was amazing. I was a believer before then, but now.....everything will be different."

"What do you mean? What could be different if you already knew Jesus?"

"I've been doing it by faith all these years, Nate. I knew about Jesus, and I knew about trusting him for my salvation, and I had a relationship with him in a small way. But to see spiritual reality is like entering another world. It's like seeing sound or hearing love or holding the wind in your hand to examine it. I knew it was there, but then it was....there. I know when I get back home the Scriptures are going to have new meaning for me..... And I'm going to have fun trying to explain what happened here."

Nate thought a moment then said with resolution,

"I can't deny in any way what happened here. The love I felt when Jesus was talking to Shamus was realer than real.....You think we'll be branded as fanatics?"

"What we've seen and experienced here is supposed to be normal. The Scriptures say that eye has not seen nor ear heard about and has not entered into the heart of a man the things God has prepared for those who love him. If anything, those who don't believe us will have the problem."

"Isaac....you think Jesus will show up in The Village like he did here?"

"Why would Jesus give us something like that and take it away? Nope, I think it's up to us to take it with us and be crazy enough to share it with the others. Let the chips fall where they may."

Dodee and Maria spent the early morning reading Papa's word to the flock and enjoying the consequential chats, while Nate and Isaac were on their way back to Grindlay Village. They should return the following afternoon.

Roee, Shamus, Jacob and Rigo were looking over the rough-sketch cabin plans Roee had put together from his vision. They had enough experience amongst them to pull off most of the construction. What they lacked would take creative thinking.

Their immediate objective was the constructing of the foundation and interior hearth. With rocks in abundance, only mortar was needed for holding them together and filling gaps against unwanted critters. Jacob and Rigo would return home right away for sufficient quantity to lay the foundation and use for chinking between the logs.

While there, they would pick up plywood for the roof, roofing felt and nails. If there was time, they would share a report of the good things that were going on.

A round trip should take a long day to load the two trucks and return.

With Jacob and Rigo away, Roee had the freedom to nurture a father-like relationship with Shamus. He could teach him about faith while they worked on leveling uneven ground for the foundation and fireplace. He would launch his emphasis with addressing what it meant to be baptized.

"Shamus," began Roee. "When Jesus went into you, he began the process of making you into another person that has all of his characteristics. He works that transformation from the inside out. Baptism is an outward statement of agreement to let him work that process in you. It's something you do because you love him and it says you understand what he has done for you and what he is asking you to let him do in you."

"Let me make sure I'm getting what you're saying," interrupted Shamus. "Okay. Jesus reveals the truth of his love for me and wants me to love him. But he doesn't force me to do that? He lets me do that? Does he let me ask questions?"

"He loves questions and enjoys answering them. And yes, the love you willingly give him, he considers the best kind of love to receive from you. What else?"

"Last night when he entered into me, you're saying he made me a new person. Or did he just start making me a new person?"

"Both Shamus. You are now and becoming a new man."

"Well, I feel like a new man. There's stuff that is gone that was there and stuff that is there I didn't have before. So that's the new man thing?"

"Yup. Also, when you are baptized, you are essentially showing your agreement with Jesus' crucifixion and resurrection for yourself."

"I don't think I understand that part," responded Shamus.

"When Jesus died on the cross, he died so you won't be stuck with your old life. That old life died last night. You agree that the man you used to be is now dead and buried. That's what symbolically happens when you go down into the water."

"That's my history you were talking about? All that I was? All the stuff I've done to myself and others? That's.....that's dead?"

"That's it Shamus. For the most part, you got it. We'll talk about others later."

"When Jesus was resurrected from the dead, he was given a new body that would never die again. Because of his resurrection, you will outlive your existing body and every problem you come up against in this life on earth. Your soul will never die. You've been given a gift of a new life with God from this moment forward. Death and problems are no longer something to fear."

"And that is my destiny? To live as though I will never die?"

"That is just the beginning. Learning to live with Jesus and like Jesus lived is a process of letting Papa work that life into you. And while you're here and beyond, you live that relationship as a son in his family."

"I'm a son?" Shamus was now completely excited.

"Yes, he adopted you and put his name on you. He does that to everyone who chooses him as their Papa. It's like saying: 'Shamus, a son of God'"

"And being baptized means I agree to let that happen in my life?"

"That's what it means. You're done with your past and accepting your future."

Shamus thought about all that for a few seconds, then added, "Why wouldn't I want to be baptized. When can I do that?"

"We just need to find or create a deep enough place to do it."

"There's a little pool behind the waterfall back up

the road we came in on."

"I've never seen a waterfall near here," marveled Roee.

"Yeah, it comes down off a high place next to the road. There's a bunch of rocks stacked up there like a dam and the water backs up behind it. It looks like someone built it."

"That's interesting," mused Roee. "Tell you what we can do. When the guys bet back, we'll have a baptism. I think Nate will want to do it, too. And I'm sure Jacob and Rigo would love to be a part of it with you."

Roee and Shamus worked all day to clear and level an area for the foundation, hearth, fireplace and future addition.

With the return of Jacob and Rigo came the beginning of evening's twilight.

The four would spend the first part of the next day gathering various sized rocks. By midday they were measuring, laying out and squaring the four walls of the foundation. By evening, the first layer of stonework was in place with the interior part of the hearth roughly shaped. The outside fireplace and chimney pad would begin when the log walls were complete.

About sunset, Isaac and Nate arrived with their first load from the Village. Remaining a day to help, they headed for another load.

While the men were busy building a foundation for the house, Dodee and Maria formed a foundation of what would be a long relationship. From the moment Maria stepped out of Rigo's truck, affinity clicked in with them; like they had always been friends. Kindred hearts spent little of their initial time together careful about potential offences and tender spots. They intuitively knew where they could venture.

Dodee foresaw the men locking into project focus, so she whisked Maria away for a walk. Their stroll took them to the pasture and on toward Vision Rock. Small talk quickly forged into openness.

Maria and Rigo's roots were planted in South America; their parents immigrating at different times to Texas while they were young. Meeting when both were occupied with the mohair industry, they had married ten years prior. And like Roee and Dodee, they were still childless but hopeful. Maria still spoke with a slight Spanish accent, which for sentimental reasons she didn't want to correct like Rigo had.

"Rigo and I saved enough money for a down payment on a ranch near Little Faith. We had heard about the beginnings of a goat industry there and saw the potential of doing well if we got involved while it was still young. We felt we could influence it into a larger direction."

"Del and Kathy really know their stuff about milking goats but little about mohair. By working together, we hope to create better markets for all of us. Have you given any thought to shearing your Angoras for their hair?"

"We know nothing about Angora goats, Maria. We were planning to stud and start milking our young Nubians when we lived in Grindlay Village. But we have little knowledge about how to care for these Angoras. The life we have here is still new. But we would love any help you want to give us. And I'm sure we can work together to get it to market."

"The most important question we face is about why we are here. Papa's direction and calling was so obvious. And now that we have decided to stay, we need the next piece of the puzzle."

"I would be happy to teach you about mohair Dodee. It's a very specialized niche. And if done right can be profitable. But could there be more concerns to this matter than shearing twice a year?"

The two laughed about the obvious.

"Yeah," responded Dodee. "These are not your normal Angoras are they? They talk and have a heart to love God. That means they should have a say about this type of stuff. And we can't manipulate a right response."

"I have an idea, Dodee. It's like a connection between what we are doing in Lawless and what you are doing here. Maybe better said, it is a connection between what God is doing in Lawless and what he is doing here."

"We want to see the street girls in Lawless come to Jesus. If they have a safe place to go where the traffickers can't find them, they can build new lives and get healed of their past without fear of being forced to go back. Right now, we don't have a place like that."

"Maria, that's an idea with a lot of potential. I wonder how a talking goat community could help these girls?"

"Oh Dodee, these people don't have an understanding of normal and don't trust anyone human. Perhaps they could learn trust from someone who does not have a personal agenda for them."

"Like goats," they both said in unison and then laughed.

"What's more, Dodee. We can give them a skill. If we can give them something they want to be good at, we can give them hope and a sense of purpose and a road away from their old life. It's a starting place."

"The mohair industry is more than just shearing, its yarn and clothing and rugs. And believe it or not, even teddy bears. They can learn any part of this industry and we can teach them to creatively build on it."

"Some of what you're saying," responded Dodee, "might be a ways off in development. But I know Roee. He will come up with something to get started. He just needs to know more about it."

"First, we need to ask Papa about this. And if he is in it we will have a talk with the goats."

"I love that you call God "Papa," remarked Maria. "It's not something I have heard of before. Tell me how you have come to do that."

"I'd love to Maria. And the basic reason is so simple. We are God's sons and daughters. So it should be natural to call him Father. In Romans chapter eight, it says we have the spirit of adoption through which we call him 'Daddy' or 'Papa.' I have grown a lot in my Father's love over the years. It is increasingly intimate. And he has encouraged me to call him Papa because he loves me like that and wants me to know how close he is with me. After all, doesn't he live inside us?"

"Yes, of course," responded Maria. "But what about reverence for God?"

"Our world's cultures have redefined reverence to mean distance, Maria. Jesus said to come to him as little children. In my child-likeness I have a lot of respect and admiration for him, but I also get to climb up in his lap and have a snuggle. He wants me to be near him and ask questions about who he is and what he does and how he does it."

"You could call him Father or God if that helps you to be close to him, there's nothing wrong with that. To me, Father seems so formal and closed off from me, like I have to be careful. Papa or Daddy is open hearted and honest. So I have the freedom to talk to him about anything anywhere and know it will be a loving and sincere conversation......even a fun one. That's who he is, Maria. That's part of what he died and rose again to give us. I know if I were to say something irreverent he would lovingly correct me. He's my Papa."

"I like that, Dodee. I like that a lot."

Dodee let Maria muse for a moment.

"My earthly father and I didn't have a relationship like that. I guess I still see God more distant because of it."

"Would you like to talk about it? What was it like with your father?"

"He is a good man. But in South America, we were very poor. In desperation, he sold me to a wealthy ranchero to be a servant, a slave if you really want to be accurate. My father said he would come back for me soon, but I did not hear from my father after that for three years. And for a young little girl it was a horribly long time. I was so lonely. It hurt my heart very deeply and I truly believed my father abandoned me."

Tears came to Maria's eyes. Dodee put her arm around her shoulder for comfort.

"Then one day he came for me and we soon left the country. I know it must have been hard for him to sell me. But he never wanted to talk about it or say he was sorry or ask my forgiveness. He didn't seem to grasp the damage he'd done or he was afrid to bring it up. And now....now we do not have a close relationship. It is very distant and he is satisfied with that."

"Have you forgiven him?"

"Many times with my words. But I cannot talk to

him about it. So in my heart maybe not."

"As you have seen Maria, this valley is gifted with a very special presence. From that presence love creates extraordinary miracles. Would you like to pray with me?"

"Yes Dodee. Please. I want my heart to be free."

Dodee smiled and closed her eyes for a moment. She found a starting thought.

"Maria, I want you to picture yourself back in slavery in a familiar room somewhere on the rancho. What do you see?"

She thought briefly before speaking.

"I am in my room and by myself. I'm feeling very alone and feeling like no one cares."

"Jesus, please come and be with Maria right now."

"Now what do you see, Maria?"

"I feel his presence."

Caught up in the moment, Maria turned around as if looking for someone. Without making a full circle she stopped and smiled broadly.

"I see him. I am not alone. Jesus, you are so beautiful. He is walking toward me. He is pointing to a knife handle in my chest."

A brief scream and Maria fell sobbing on the green grass.

Dodee sat next to her to wait for Holy Spirit to work his healing.

"He says he is taking my griefs, Dodee. He takes my sorrows and puts them on his shoulders."

"He removed the knife from my heart, and He told me: 'I paid for your healing and freedom with my death, Maria.' And now he is showing me my pain and unforgiveness inside the scars of his hands. I can see it and it is ugly. He said: 'I make everything beautiful at the right time. This is your time, Maria.' And as I forgive my father his scars are returning to the beautiful offerings they were."

Dodee reached for Maria's hand. "Peace, Maria. I bless you with shalom rav; deep peace and well being."

Maria's face resembled the effect of a liquid being poured over her. Every part of her relaxed as something unseen flowed down her entire body. She slipped into Dodee's arms.

Maria offered a single word in affectionate response. "Papa."

On the night of Isaac and Nate's return, faces human and goat reflected the light from the campfire. Small talk about the day's activities waned to a peaceful quietness and the singing of heart-felt songs of worship took their place.

After that, the moment was at hand for Roee to

bring up a topic for family discussion.

"Shamus and I have had opportunity to talk about baptism while you guys were gone. And I've been looking forward to this chance to share what we talked about."

"For the sake of the flock, Nate and anyone else who wants to hear, I want to tell you the nature and substance of baptism."

For several minutes, Roee painted the picture of baptism's significance as discussed with Shamus.

"We've been waiting for everyone to be present so Shamus could be baptized. And I was thinking Nate might want to join in. Isaac, Jacob and Rigo could be here as witnesses. Any thoughts on that?"

"Yeah Roee," Nate responded. "It was a defining moment. My life will never be the same since the night Jesus showed up here. I'm a new man, too. I want to do this."

"I want to be baptized too, Roee," inserted Maria.

"You were baptized years ago Maria," declared Rigo. "You don't need to do it again."

"That was a mere formality back then Rigo. My encounter with him today killed a part of the old me that was not yet dead. Or better yet, a part of me that was dead is now alive. And my heart's picture of who he is has changed because I have seen him. As of today, I am different in ways I don't have words for."

"Yes mi amor, I see it in your eyes....and your smile."

"This is a special moment," she said as she put her hands to her heart. "It is the perfect way to express it."

With tears of joy for his wife's new freedom, Rigo gave his sincere blessing, "Sigue tu corazon, Maria."

Willie brought up an challenging question.

"Do us goats need to be baptized?"

Roee chuckled because of the uncertainty of what his answer should be.

"You guys have a very unique function in Papa's design. He created and called you for a specific purpose and promised you a place in heaven like us humans. Do you remember, Willie? He said he has never done it before and will not do it again. Somehow, he has given you a gift to live for his purposes similar to the angels in design. Unless Papa shows me different, I don't see any spiritual requirement for you guys to be baptized. Is that okay?"

Willie got a mischievous look on his face, chuckled and said, "Sure, I'm okay with that. Where are we going to have this baptism?"

"Shamus said there's a little waterfall with a pool behind it back up the road toward town."

"There's no waterfall back there," declared Tanny with certainty. "Never has been."

"And there isn't a road there either," insisted Willie.

"You wouldn't suppose," speculated Roee, "that little earthquake we had the other day might explain something?"

"In the morning, we will go have a baptism and see what other unusual surprises Papa has in store for us."

The morning parade was peculiar as Shamus and Jacob lead the way to the waterfall with a flock of goats and eight humans. There was a dozen conversations going, so not only was it odd it was noisy.

The marvel of seeing the falls was accompanied by the fact that neither the road nor the rock dam were there just three days before.

"This is so weird," exclaimed Roee. "The landscape looks like this corridor has been here for years. And the stonework looks like it's been intentionally stacked recently to create this dam."

"I've been by this way three times. Twice when I followed Finny and once when I brought Finny and Megan back from the east. This area was entirely forested."

"I remember something Jesus said when we ran into him at the beginning," remarked Jacob. "He said, 'It's almost like it was made just for you.' You know, I have never seen one miracle before I came to this place. And now it's like they're a way of life."

"Jacob," declared Roee, "I believe it is Papa's intention for you all to take that understanding back to your homes and use it to show his great and wonderful love. This valley is alive with his life and he wants everyone in the world to experience it whether they come here or not."

"But hey, we're here to have baptisms. Papa made this little pool just so you guys could be dunked! It just doesn't get any better than that! And it saves me the labor of building a pond. I might even raise some fish in this.....Thank you, Papa."

Roee and Jacob then proceeded to baptize Shamus. And as he came out of the water he wept over thoughts about where his life was headed and declared, "I'm a new man and my old life is dead! And good riddance to it. I hope I never see that guy again."

Getting out of the water he stood reflecting on the commitment he had just made and watched as the others entered in. As he quietly prayed, he started muttering words that nobody around him understood.

Nate was next, then Maria, both having their moment of engagement with Papa's heart.

As people cleared the water Sully made a running leap from the side, landing clumsily in the water. It was just the encouragement the others needed to follow in after him. Although a baptism of fun, it caught Papa's attention. The flock was making unspoken statements of commitment. Revelry took over the group as shouts, whoops and other expressions of delight captivated the atmosphere. It was a wonder Shamus didn't get trampled in the excitement.

Dodee leaned into Roee, "I have never in my life seen a goat swim or even want to get in water like that."

In time, laughter subsided, Shamus recovered and the train of man and critter headed back toward home with the young ones talking and playing at the rear.

And once again, Rigo spotted movement in the undergrowth to the rear. He slowed his pace to let the kids catch up with the main flock while he kept watch behind.

"Come on guys, stay together."

It wasn't easy to drum up the desire to start work after the boisterous festivities of the morning. It would be much easier to bask in Papa's presence for the remainder of the day and be lazy. But even working in his presence was a special act of worship. So with extra resolve, construction began anew.

The remainder of that day and the next, saw the completion and leveling of the foundation and hearth. The next morning Nate and Isaac were off again for another round of moving what they could from the Grindlay house.

For another three days, work was focused on breaking out the chain saws to cut trees and mill planks for the floor.

On the second morning of this phase Nate and

Isaac returned with their load from the house. As before, they would remain one day to help then make another trip. The system was gaining a rhythm.

On the fourth day trees for the walls were felled and dragged to the foundation with the trucks. The fifth and sixth days saw the crucial first layers of walls installed with slow precision. The following layers were slightly quicker.

In the course of that first week, Shamus engaged his heart in the bonds of trusted friendships and mentoring while he experienced the satisfaction of creating something.

Jacob and Rigo learned about Roee's capacity to be a regular guy when he hit his thumb and finger with a hammer and squashed his hand under a heavy log. The guys marveled at what pain could do to a grown man's composure.

Nate and Isaac were grateful for the opportunity they had been unwittingly thrust into. Their time in Wonder Valley was the seed of a planting for Papa to extend his pleasure and presence to Grindlay Village.

Maria and Dodee bonded deeper and were thriving at teaching goat school. The goats were getting comfortable talking with humans and memorizing. The framework of a community was taking shape.

The seventh day came and Roee proclaimed a very welcomed rest day. It was a hard reminder to discover how much work a project was without the ease of modern tools. The men were not only tired, but sore from heavy lifting, the result of not having a small crane to position the logs.

Roee was looking forward to a few hours alone up on the rock. But, it appeared that plan was not to be realized.......at least not today.

Before Roee could reach the edge of the pasture just below the last ascent to the rock, he heard yelling voiced in his direction and using his name. What he saw was three new men standing with the others; everyone beckoning with their hands for him to return.

The longing in his heart and the ache in his muscles pulled on him to ignore their cries and continue the other way.

As Roee arrived, introductions were made.

The story about these men was they were brothers and shepherds of sheep who live with families in a mountain valley thirty miles to the south. A man in camouflage clothing appeared to them in dreams they all had on the same night and told them about what was going on to the north. He gave them Roee's name and beckoned them to go and help build a cabin.

Because of the location of their valley the journey required they descend to the lower valley before ascending to this place. The process put them in contact with Nate and Isaac while they were home loading for another trip.

What made them especially helpful was they had experience building several cabins and knew their craft well. Their experience was strategic help for this phase of the project.

Instead of rest, work ramped up in greater earnest. With walls at their current height the extra laborers and experience to raise the logs to their notches was a welcome addition.

With the extra help and tools they brought with them the walls were finished and roof beams, rafters and collar ties in place by the time the three brothers needed to return to their flocks.

They had stories to take home; stories of talking goats, loving neighbors, demonstrations of spiritual activity and testimonies of miracles. Their desire to hear and experience more was overruled by their need to tend to waiting responsibilities. They committed themselves to return when they had a break after fall shearing and left directions about where and how to find them if any of the Wonder Valley group should have opportunity to make a visit south. Once again seeds were planted in those who would take this life elsewhere.

For a second time Roee called for a day to rest before finishing the roof. All the men were near exhaustion. Isaac and Nate returned home to spend a few days with their families and catch up on chores. And the group from Little Faith would remain to nail down the roof. That night the others went to their tents early while Roee and Shamus hung around the campfire. Roee was tired, but it appeared Shamus wanted to talk.

"Roee, the last few weeks have been the most incredible weeks of my life."

"In what way Shamus?"

"I don't think I have the kind of words that would say everything I'm feeling. But I'll try."

After a pause to search his thoughts, he continued. "I've made a lot of money from the old life I had. But now, I'm wealthy in ways I never thought a man could be wealthy."

"I've been around a lot of unsavory people, and even created a family of them on the street. But I've never known family like I know it today. For the first time in my life, I belong. I have a father and mother and brothers and sisters. I feel loved and I can actually give away love in some small way."

"Sounds to me," responded Roee, "like you found the right words, Shamus."

"Yeah, I guess I did," responded Shamus with a smile and resumed his thoughts. "Jake, Rigo and Maria will be going back in a couple of days. And I want to ask you if I can stay with you and Dodee. I have so much to learn still."

"Shamus, you can stay as long as you want and we'd love to have you. Is there anything you need from Lawless?"

"There's not much there worth having. Maybe just some practical stuff. But someday I want to return to tell them what Papa has done for me. Maybe I can bring some of them back here to be around talking goats and all the life that lives here. They deserve an encounter like I had. They deserve the healing I'm getting. They deserve to be loved like I'm being loved."

"I know someday soon," started Roee, "your heart and spirit will be empowered to return to Lawless and show them the kind of love you've been given. Some will say yes to your invitation and some will not. You will need to love them enough to let them make that decision."

"For now, Papa is revealing your destiny and what it means to live it. Your design as a son as you get to know it, will help you understand how you relate to Papa. And as you grow in that he will uniquely train you in how to affect the world for his purposes."

"The long and the short of it is, I would count it an honor to have you here and teach you God's ways for as long as Papa would have us do that. I have a feeling Papa is going to use these goats to open your eyes to things as well. It will be a fun adventure to have you help us unpack what he's doing here."

"Yeah," said Shamus with a yawn. "I can only imagine. It seems like a lot."

"Thank you. Thanks for letting me stay."

"I'm sorry Roee, would you mind if I went to my tent? I'm exhausted."

"I'm right behind you on that."

As Shamus wandered to bed, the embers of the fire reflected the warmth of Roee's heart and his affection for the wonder of Papa's redemption.

"Papa, you take delight in your people and crown the humble with salvation.

Who am I that you would take me out of the darkness of this world and show me your light?

Who am I that you would write my name in your book?

Who am I that you remember me?

Who am I that you watch over me?

Who am I that you know me in every detail?

Who am I that you have placed such a high value on my life?

Who am I that you would make me your habitation?"

"Papa, I am blessed beyond measure. Thank you for such great abundance"

ALMOST NORMAL

The cabin stood substantially complete as a basic form. While the roof was in want of a finished covering in the event of a storm, it was decently raintight. Although laying the courses of stonework for the fireplace and chimney would continue steadily, its services as a heating source would not be required for a few months. And cooking would continue as it had. Doors and windows were covered with temporary treatments to keep the flying creatures out until frames and glass could be installed.

Thanks to the trips Nate and Isaac made to bring furnishings from the Grindlay house, the new one had the rustic backwoods feel transferred from there. Minimally equipped with human comforts it was livable and a fine home.

Nate and Isaac had been two of a crew who willingly sowed into the foundation of what would be called the Wonder Valley culture. Now tired and satisfied for their labors of love, they returned home where they would reap a harvest of Kingdom gold, silver and precious incense. The impartation to them of the song embedded in Wonder Valley extended Papa's reach to their region.

Their labors galvanized that peculiarly magical bond typical of people working side by side. As they dovetailed into one mind through intuitive anticipation of the needs and actions of the project, they worked efficiently to accomplish the mundane and difficult.

Satisfaction in a job well done contributed to a deeper meaning of teamwork. A foundational framework of camaraderie and lasting friendship was also constructed in the process of building this home for Roee and Dodee. This too would weather storms and prove its mettle.

Roee's fresh season of consistent and extended times with sunrises and waiting with Papa for spiritual renewal, focus and direction brought a welcomed restoration of his favorite pursuits. Questions would have time to form well and answers would have the opportunity to grow wide with wisdom. For the moment, life was normal.

While Roee looked for heavenly reflection and intimacy outdoors, Dodee found it around her preferred domain in the cabin. She enjoyed the creative challenges to her spirit of nurturing an atmosphere within her home to form the precious restorative refuge it was. Hosting Papa's presence inside and out made everything work the way it was created to.

It hadn't been long since Maria wandered from her farm home and stumbled into Wonder Valley, which was now home base to a one-of-a-kind spiritual something. It now fell to the shepherds to critically analyze current understanding and prepare for the next step. The scrutiny of it was elusive. And its activity unparalleled under the watchful eye of any historical revivalism.

What the shepherds didn't know was Papa had initiated the next phase through the departure of the cabin builders. It was Papa's fruit and he was creatively growing it well in a cloud of mystery.

But how does one prepare for the unexpected? The extended answer to this question has a story to tell about creating culture, a new state of ordinary and a new shape of normal.

It didn't take Roee and Dodee long to figure out the prevailing purpose and design. They would continue to cultivate an environment of love and seek to create a new culture that now included talking goats, ragtag and sundry humans, supernatural events and heavenly beings. What could be more normal than that?

Other facets surrounding their analysis had yet to achieve a state of clarity. Finishing their shift in thinking from ordinary people to extraordinary would helpfully add important ingredients to their confidence in solving the unknowns.

Peeling away the layers about this enigma began in the forest during Roee's initial pursuit of Maria. He was unaware of how much of that mystery was yet to unpack; it extended far beyond the canvas of the immediate portrait. And the portal that energized its genesis in the forest was now a vortex in the valley. It drew more life into its life, only to randomly jettison its bi-product of power without seemingly understandable design into the outlying countryside. Through the rings of its associated ripple effect, the extended reach was indeterminable. As it became the norm, it was now unstoppable.

During morning breakfast in the cabin, Shamus asked a light-hearted question.

"Now that I'm here with you guys, does this make me a goat herder in training?"

"There is another alternative," stated Roee. "You could become a goat."

"Have you had any strong urges to eat unusual things lately?" queried Dodee straight-faced.

"That's funny," responded Shamus good naturedly.

"I think I hear what you're asking," began Roee more seriously. "What is our purpose in living in this valley?"

"Here we are, hours from anything civilized. We have the distinct privilege of a spiritual presence that many people who love Papa would sell everything they own to be a part of. And yet, for some reason, a flock of goats sovereignly chosen by God appear to be the key players in an unknown outcome of what is happening here."

"Obviously, we don't know what we need to know to make a more accurate game plan about where we are going and how we will get there. But there are two assumptions we can make without reservation. And the rest may have to be filled in as we go."

"The first and most important thing we can take for granted is that Jesus wants everyone in the world to be with him in heaven. The only way they can get there is for us to tell them about his great and deep love. And expose them to the supernatural wonders and signs that make his message impossible to ignore."

"We can, of course, do that part without talking goats who have seen heaven and been with Jesus. But whenever I think of that, I see a clear picture of Jesus laughing hilariously. I think he enjoys offending religious and supposedly wise minds, including mine. The fact that I can't think of a good reason for it is probably wrapped around the possibility of its simplicity. It's hidden in the obvious. I may end up filing that under "duh" when I finally see its true value to God."

"Allow me to consider this," insisted Shamus. "If it weren't for those goats, I wouldn't be here talking with you. I would still be hustling johns for tricks with the ladies I enslaved. I would still be a hopeless empty shell of a soul without meaning."

"And there's still a thousand guys like me out there that need what I have; an encounter with God that never stops. When I go back I hope I can take a couple of goats to help me talk to them."

"Roee, that city to the north you've talked about makes Lawless look like a ski resort. People come to Lawless to play. In Burnus, they take play seriously. If you don't do their game their way, you die. It will take something powerful to break into their darkness, Roee."

"Nothing," responded Roee. "Nothing is too difficult for Papa. He has the keys to death and hell. He has reached cities and nations before and he will do it again. And it may be that he will use you and some very special goats to do it."

"When the time comes for that to happen, we will be ready and Papa will make it happen. So long as we see him as King, we will be where we need to be and when we need to be there."

As Roee spoke, he studied Shamus' eyes. In them was a passion and joy for the one who saved him from what would have undoubtedly been the irreversible and complete corruption of his soul. The intervention he experienced was opening his heart to reach those who are like what he was. From the first time of their meeting he had felt Papa's love for this man. And now, he would always picture him in the arms of Jesus at a campfire setting.

"Getting back to my train of thought....."

"Another factor was drawn from a vision I had before I showed up in Lawless. I was up on the rock above the valley praying about the building of a home for Dodee and myself. He showed me the design of our cabin and how to build it."

"Then he took me up in the air. I can't tell you if what I saw was real or if it was vision; it was all the same to me. I could see the farms out to the east where Lawless is, and the city to the north of here, which you say is named Burnus. I saw clearly to the west and south. He told me he was going to bring his servants to help build this house. And as you know, they have come from every direction but north."

"In saying he would help build this physical cabin he added that he wanted me to pray for the building of his house. His house is people, and it will take huge numbers of people to fill it."

"The Bible says that heaven is Papa's throne and earth is his foot rest. There isn't a house big enough to contain God. According to Carrie, heaven makes our universe look like a peanut. In metaphor, it tells us that no matter how big and out of reach the darkness appears to us, the light of our God is vastly greater."

"What I understand of that is, we are to seek the lost and invite them into his house. We are to show them with authentic love and convincing signs and wonders that he cares for them. With all the creative ways he makes that available to us we apparently need this valley of his presence to spearhead the task."

"We are vitalized through the song of life and love sung in every element of creation here. It continually draws us closer to Papa. From his presence and with his presence, he sends us wherever he purposes to go. And when we return, we come back to this place of refreshing, made fresh again by the wellspring of living water available to us."

Roee paused briefly.

"Now that I think about it, both assumptions are

actually one. The first he has told everyone to do. The second is our personal assignment as sons of the Great King. Does that sound like something you want to be a part of Shamus?"

Shamus looked at Roee with careful deliberation before answering.

"I was really looking forward to being a goat herder, Roee."

As they laughed, Roee responded, "Sorry for the downgrade."

"Seriously Roee, you inspire me deeply and count me in with what will play out here. But I know I have a lot to learn. And I feel like there are doors to the past that need to be closed."

"Your original question about goat herding provokes some thought, Shamus. I've learned a lot about people as a goat herder. When Papa assigned me to taking care of goats, I was offended by the idea of it. It was below my social station. I had a hard time with it. And for awhile, I rejected it. I was highly trained in another field and proud of my talents and abilities; caught up with my self-importance."

"After awhile, I discovered that Papa uses what appears to be foolish things to humble the so-called wise and learned; such as myself. And through a willing heart to be faithful with the small things he's given me he can now entrust me with greater things. In my case it's more goats."

"But as you know, not your average goats. These goats were hidden away in this valley for generations. Shepherds came and went, preparing a legacy for them to be revealed when the time was right. In the book of Proverbs, a man named Agar calls the ants 'a people who are beyond wise,' preparing for what is ahead. Until recently, I would not have said that goats were a wise people, if people at all. But through my experiences with them, I see them differently. I see them through the eyes of love and understand them for their need, not their failings. They simply need a shepherd who will love them and see them for who they are created to be. That understanding changes the way I encounter people."

"Shamus, there are lessons to be learned through these goats that will prepare you to return to Lawless and shepherd the people there into a new life."

"These same goats are instruments and conduits for the purposes and power of an amazingly wise Father. He isn't looking for the best and most qualified to redeem humankind. He is looking for humble and loving goats who will be real, courageously obey him, show up and let him do the work."

"Probably over-simplified," said Roee with a smile.

"I guess," pondered Shamus, "being a goat herder can be enlightening."

"Oh absolutely! And more than that, there are degrees in goat herding you know. I almost have my GHD. Then I can put 'Doctor' in front of my name."

"GHD?"

"Well, yeah, Goat Herder Dude."

Shamus and Dodee looked at each other and shook their heads.

"With that bit of humor, it will be good to go spend some time with them."

"Building the cabin was a huge investment of time as far as they were concerned. I'd like to find out how they fared with all the new people coming and going. It must have been challenging."

"Anyone care to join me?"

"You guys go on, Doctor Goatman, GHD," stated Dodee with a smile and a bow. "I'll be out after I clean up a bit."

Roee blew a ram's horn to call the goats together and for the purpose of giving them a treat. To hear the small trumpet blast rejoin off the hills and surrounding cliffs was delightful. The unique timbre lingered as it pierced the length and width of the valley and brought every creature great and small to attention. But only the goats knew its true significance.......treats!

Today Roee and Shamus brought wet COB, a mixture of corn, oats and barley with a touch of molasses; to give each one a handful. In a normal flock, a snack of COB would provoke an unbridled and greedy feeding frenzy. But this flock was learning there would always be enough and gave place to let others go first.

The growing love culture among this tribe was producing deepening excellence. Patience, kindness, keeping short accounts of things done wrong and finding happiness in watching the positive progress of others allowed the flock to experience the dynamics of family on expanding levels. Peculiar behavior for a goat herd.

As the goats sauntered toward them, Roee and Shamus fed each one a handful of wet COB from a small dish, stroked them lovingly and jested with them affectionately. With the flock fully present, Roee then had Shamus narrate a chapter from the book of Revelation where it talks about heaven and angels.

"Anybody have any thoughts or questions about that?" asked Roee.

"We're not alone here in the valley Papa Shepherd," responded Rosie. "I see angels almost all the time. One of them told me that some of them are here to protect us and others come to bring praise to this place. I'm getting quite comfortable with them around. It's almost normal."

"It seems," continued Roee, "our unexpected launch into heaven created quite a change. As seeing angels becomes normal, we may have the privilege of seeing and hearing other things. These events seem to give us confidence about the invisible things around us.

"Carrie told us when she was here we all have a personal angel. And as Finnegan, Megan and I experienced when we had our encounter with Nara on our return trip, there are protective angels that fight for us when needed. Rosie, your report verifies those things."

"Nara is still around, you know," stated Sully with concern. "When Rigo was here, he told me of two sightings. Once, he put himself between Nara and some of our young ones to protect them. What are we going to do about him?"

"First thing you all need to know," answered the shepherd, "is we have nothing to be afraid of. What happened to Carrie is proof we have no reason to fear. Even if Nara were to kill any of us, where would we be?"

"We would be in heaven with Carrie," responded Maria. "That wouldn't be a bad thing as far as I'm concerned."

"And I was there," stated Willie, "when Mama Shepherd raised her back to life. That was pretty amazing. Can you teach us to do that?"

"That part is simple, Willie," said Roee. "Jesus does it all. He raises from death. He gives healing to bodies. He has all ability to change spiritual moods in the air. And he runs off critters like Nara with a single word; no argument necessary. And he does it because he loves each and every one of us. The simplicity of the doing is in this: agree with what Papa wants to do and speak it out for him."

Roee could tell by the confident buzz of voices around the flock most if not all of the goats understood and believed what he said.

"Secondly, no matter what you feel at any time, the truth is he wants to express his love and compassion powerfully. It's your bold love for him and your understanding of his deep love for others that allows him to do it through you."

"What's compassion?" asked Rosie.

"You are compassion, Rosie," responded Papa Shepherd with a warm smile. "You see those who suffer, you feel their pain and want to do something about it."

"And now I can do something about it!" declared Rosie excitedly. "I got it! I get it! Mama Shepherd told us that Jesus is with us all the time. He never goes away, ever! If he is always with us, so is his power to do all these things when humans or goats are suffering! That is the greatest thing I have ever heard!"

Once again, the voicing of the flock indicated truth had been revealed to the heart and understood. And with the acceptance of truth, came the life-giving activation of it.

By late evening Shamus headed for his tent filled with an instructive day on spiritual issues and observations into the family dynamics of goats. Surrounded by a healthy family had proven to be a vital key to unlocking healings of his traumatic past. His childhood affected him in so many ways by things that should have happened but didn't. And more frequently than ought to be, things that shouldn't have happened but did.

With the healing process working its wonders, the little boy that didn't get to grow up normally was feeling genuine happiness. Not the artificial happiness that ebbed and flowed with the pursuit of pleasures and possessions or positions and status. But the contentment and rock solid stability of knowing he was unconditionally loved no matter the circumstances of life or his ability to get everything right.

As he sank onto his cot and into his sleeping bag, he looked up and said: "You did all of this for me. Thank you, Papa. Thank you, thank you and thank you."

Marveling at the thought of being grateful, he considered the entitlement thinking and selfishness it had displaced. He smiled and began to laugh. Papa's presence flooded his tent as he opened his child-like arms for a good night kiss from his heavenly Daddy. "Thanks for adopting me. I love having a nice home."

Roee slipped into bed next to Dodee with a tired sigh. The day had not been physically challenging. Although, it was great to take a break from the heavy lifting and hard work of building the cabin, the rewarding work of personal involvement left a different and satisfying weariness.

The pause allowed his mind to contemplate creatively and more like a shepherd. As Roee and Dodee laid in bed, Roee put his hands behind his head, briefly wishing he had a view of the stars.

"I've been wondering about these goats, love."

"Well," responded Dodee playfully, "Wonder Valley is a good place for wondering. I can't imagine what an expert goat herder with a GHD could possibly be wondering about. Tell me Doctor Goatman, what high-level curiosities have been on your mind?"

Roee rolled over chuckling at her sarcastic humor. Wearing a smile that would illuminate the room if white teeth and warmth of heart could glow in the dark, he put his arm around her; gently pulling her close. She responded with a hug of her own.

"I've been thinking about the next generation of goats. Papa said what he is doing is unique to this tribe. What I don't know....because Papa didn't say for sure.... is if the new babies will have the same gifts and calling as the ones who have had the visitation. Are we going to repopulate the earth with talking goats? Or is it just for this generation? What do you think, Doctor Watson? Do you have any clues about this mystery?"

Using her best and actually quite good British accent, she gave an animated and mock thoughtful reply.

"Well I'm not an expert on supernaturally inclined goats, Mister Holmes. I leave that complex stuff to deep thinkers like yourself. But I am an expert on what it would take to have a baby daughter. So I plead with you sir, to give that idea some careful examination if you please."

"How could I resist such heartfelt sincerity?"

And with that response, a quite unrelated mystery sought a solution.

Shadow of Death

The sun completed its journey beyond the horizon several hours previously and the night sky was now enhancing its joy with the appearance of the large grin of the first quarter moon. The light from its face postured above the eastern tree tops and created long, furry shadows from the pines and cedars.

Most of the flock was bedded down and sleeping. A few were still awake, standing and chewing their cud while enjoying the relaxed and cool breath of the night's breeze.

Sully, Willie, Tanny and Finnegan lounged together chatting about life and how incredibly strange the changes had affected them. Good changes had brought comfort and contentment to their once austere community.

The unexpected rend of yelling and fearful cries pierced across the pasture from the east. It was the din of mayhem and the wails of terror.

Sully, Willie, Tanny and Finnegan were on their hooves and racing bravely by the dim light of the moon toward the clamor.

From the west, Roee had quickly put on his boots and charged out with a large flashlight, leaping obstructive kids with ease. Shamus and Dodee were running behind carefully observing the flock for problems along the way.

"What's going on? Where's all the fighting?" Roee shouted while scanning left with his torch.

When Roee shouted the noise stopped. But Shamus' beam of light caught two glowing orbs to the right, crouching low about forty yards away.

Before anyone could think, Willie reacted with a dead run directly for those eyes. As Willie was about to make contact with his massive horns, Nara; blinded by Shamus' flashlight; side-stepped Willie's charge at the last second, thinking he would take him from behind as he passed by. Willie anticipated his maneuver and stopped short sweeping left with the points of his horns toward Nara. Nara dodged the attempted goring but lost his balance. Willie's reactive measure set him up for a frontal blast with his thick forehead and horns, knocking him down. Ready to easily and quickly finish Nara off with a follow-up assault; leaving nothing but the bloody cleanup; Roee authoritatively halted everything.

"That's enough Willie! Stop!"

"No!" yelled Willie, hot with anger. "I'm going to finish this!"

"There are better ways to defeat him," reasoned Roee.

Willie didn't understand Roee's reasoning, but sighed and stood down....because he trusted him.

Nara backed away from Willie a few steps and took on a calculating expression with a relaxed but "ready for anything" composure. His face was the countenance of defiance; denying the possibility of what could have been his last breath.

Shamus' big light scanned the area for casualties. Sadly, there were several. Nara had frenzied a killing spree for the pleasure of it. And he had taken down two of the young kids before the mamas stepped in to make an attempt to stop the carnage. They too were killed defending them.

"I think you're right shepherd," stated Nara with a smile, attempting to intimidate, "I've done quite well enough for one night. And unless you plan on doing something about it, it won't be the last you see of my handiwork."

"There is nothing you can do, Nara, that can't be undone. There is no scheme you can plan that can't be defeated. You will not prevail."

"It seems, shepherd," boasted Nara belligerently, "I already have."

Remarkably, it was Finny who spoke up in a passionate counter-offensive.

"We don't have to accept this! This is wrong, wrong, wrong!"

"Nara, you deceived me before when you thought you could keep me enslaved. I have lived to be free and I declare you a liar! You're nothing!"

Nara bristled at the statement and positioned himself to attack his once duped victim.

"Stand down, Nara," spoke Roee quietly, confidently and firmly, "you will do nothing."

Nara found himself unable to move. He growled scornfully at the powerlessness being forced on him.

"Papa Shepherd," said Scampy. "You said we could speak to these that are dead, and Jesus would bring them back to life! We've seen this with Carrie. And we can see it again now!"

"Yes!" exclaimed Rosie with a shout. And before Roee could respond, Rosie was at the side of the children, speaking to them to come back to life. The rest of the flock followed her example and began to speak healing and life to those who had perished. It was simple and it was passionate.

A fog of white pulsating with blue rolled up around them. Four small orbs of gold appeared, bobbing and bouncing around in the mist as if doing a ballet in the air. Their speed and intensity increased for a few minutes then shot forcefully into the bodies of the goats. The impact was electric to the atmosphere causing everyone to gasp and involuntarily jump. The four casualties reentered life sleepily, completely healed of their wounds.

With great excitement and celebration, Scampy sprung into a dance, prancing like a kid goat and singing:

"Our enemy has been defeated, death can't hold us down.

God is our strength and God is our song

We'll sing our hearts out, what a victory won!"

The others joined in the merriment repeating the song with praise and laughter.

Nara screamed at the top of his lungs, then bolted frantically into the night as if being chased.

Scampy's abundant energy and boundless enthusiasm took the worship to increased measure as the pervading mist increased in the blackness of night. With flashlights shut down, the party grew in earnest as the song of life, written and scored in this valley, swelled into an unabashed celebration.

Beings visible and invisible joined in as the valley filled with tangible awe and majestic worship of their creator. Other-worldly instruments refracted light and sound from another realm to beam through cliffs and mountains; relaying pulsing waveforms of joy through the atmosphere.

The night hours eventually gave place to changes in the morning sky. The dark scheme of night morphed to hues of azure. The glory of another sunrise brought the light of a new day's mercy and grace. The shadow of death had passed over, lost its power and left no visible aftereffects.

The intense energy of praise subsided as natural strength exhausted itself.

Shadow of Death

The hours of sleep were few, but the inner rest from the previous night's worship filled in the lack. The community managed a spark of life by mid-morning.

Willie was set on a mission for a serious talk with the shepherd. His mind was in turmoil with Roee's decision about Nara and he had questions.

Positioning himself near the trailhead leading to Vision Rock, he knew Papa Shepherd should pass in his direction shortly. His patience was rewarded with the approach of Roee.

"Good morning Willie," said Roee quietly. "You look like you have something on your mind."

"Why Papa Shepherd? We could have been rid of Nara for good if you let me finish him off. Help me understand why that wasn't a good idea. It goes against everything in my guts."

"Willie, I thought you might be troubled by that. And before I respond, I want you to know what a beautiful heart you have......courageous and selfless. You were ready to give your life for all of us if that was to be the end result of your tangle with Nara."

"I was angry and just wanted to kill him, Papa Shepherd. I was blind with rage then and maybe I still feel it. I'm not so sure what I was doing was bravery. But that doesn't change what I'm feeling today."

"I believe the answer you seek is found in the invisible....the unseen world of spirits, both evil and good. Nara is host to an evil spirit. Killing Nara doesn't destroy the spirit within him."

"Our weapons to defeat Nara are not found in our own might to destroy his body, but in our ability to defeat his power. The one who lives in us is infinitely stronger than the one that lives in him. His strength is a false strength. He has power only when he can influence someone to agree with him. He's a liar, a thief and a killer."

"His lies have power only if the lie is believed. That's what happened to Megan and Finnegan and who knows who else before that. When Finnegan and Megan believed Papa's truth, they understood the power of faith and became free of Nara's power to create doubt."

"Nara steals not because he wants possessions, but because he wants to destroy hope. If our hope and trust is not in the things of earth, he can't destroy our hope."

"Nara kills, because he wants to create fear and destroy our love. If we have no fear of death or loss, our love of life is unshakeable."

"Eventually, he will see our light as being so strong he can no longer be effective. He will move on to find easier prey or come back only if we let our guard down."

"Willie, we are the victors on this planet. It doesn't look like Super Goat against the lions. It looks like humble Willie who knows who he is and where his power comes from against an enemy who will flee when resisted."

"That idea of Super Goat sounds pretty good,

shep."

"Yeah Willie, I could see you now; huge, bulging muscles as powerful as a bear, horns sharpened to a fine edge that slice and dice your favorite foods, hooves of steel and eyes that can see for miles, ears that can hear a twig break at a hundred yards. And speed like lightning. Gosh Willie, you'd be miserable with all that power."

By the time Roee finished his list, Willie was hysterical with laughter.

Papa Shepherd let Willie enjoy the moment while he thought about where he was taking the dialogue.

"Let's take a journey with some questions Willie."

"What kind of person are you?

"I'm a goat. You know that."

"Yup, I am aware of that. But what kind of goat?"

"A long haired, long horned, stinky at times kind of goat," Willie said with a smile.

"And what is your purpose in life?"

"To eat the good things Papa has created. Rest and enjoy eating it over again in peace when I chew my cud."

"What else?"

"Bringing more goats into this world? That's a lot of fun."

"And all that makes you an ordinary goat, doesn't

it?"

"Yeah, I think that's pretty ordinary."

"But you're not ordinary, Willie. What is different about you?"

"What is different about me is what is different about all of us goats in this valley. Papa has made us into a unique breed of goat that talks with people and have a specially nice shepherd and we can raise other goats from the dead. And when we die, we will be in heaven. He said he has never done that before. So I guess that makes us Super Goats after all, doesn't it?"

This time it was Roee's turn to laugh.

"You got me there. That was brilliant Willie."

"Yeah, I know. That happens a lot lately. So do we all get special hoof coverings or something? Maybe some nice boots like you wear."

"That's funny," Roee said chuckling. "It means you're extraordinary, Willie. It also means you have a message about Papa's goodness that you can share with others."

"Will they become goats?"

"Uhhhhhh, nope. But they become a special creation like all y'all are. They will have a shepherd, be with Papa in heaven and be able to heal the sick, raise people from the dead and do a lot of special stuff that Jesus said we can do because he did."

"So what does that have to do with Nara?" Asked Willie.

"Willie, I think Papa gave you some extraordinary new brains when we went to heaven. That's an amazing question."

"I have an extraordinary teacher."

"I'm glad you think so, Willie."

"Papa didn't introduce you to heaven so you can get a glimpse of it, then sit here blissfully eating and chewing cud for the rest of your life and killing mountain lions on safari. He took you to heaven so you could see him and see what it's like. Then bring that atmosphere back here to share with those who have never experienced it."

"Nara unknowingly hates that culture. It doesn't serve his purposes. In his selfishness, he mistakenly works to stop the good life Papa wants to export from this valley. Outside of this valley, there are a thousand others like Nara doing the same thing."

Willie looked down at the grass, then pulled several bites off the top to chew on while considering Roee's words.

Roee lowered himself cross-legged to the grass and let Willie process. He knew goats do their best thinking while they eat.

Several minutes passed. Then Willie got that look on his face like he understood....that look of knowing.

"If there are a thousand like Nara spewing their death culture, then my killing Nara would mean I'm becoming like him. And whenever I run into someone like him, my response would be a mindset of death toward those people instead of a mindset of life. Not exactly the love Papa showed us."

"Nope....not exactly."

"So what I thought was your concern for Nara, is actually your concern for my heart isn't it?"

"That's a large part of it. But there's more."

Willie's eyes grew large as he considered the astonishing thought invading his mind.

"Are you trying to tell me.........that Nara could become one of us?"

THE HUNTER

Up early this morning with the arrival of summer, Roee knew Vision Rock became a Cooking Stone by late morning. The shepherd also knew the idea of frying an egg on rocks during a scorching day was myth at best; at least it was here in the valley. But heat retention in a rock substrate was a reality and he wanted no part of that while he sought to soak in the warmth of Papa's presence.

Crossing the large meadow and entering the trailhead at the edge of the forest, he slowed his pace to drink of the peaceful beauty that was prelude to reaching the Rock. As he stood drinking in the panorama he noticed that the atmosphere felt different. The birds were singing a happier song than normal.

Several squirrels were playfully tussling to his right and he greeted them with a friendly "Good morning." They stopped their circus antics to scamper toward him for a chat.

"Good morning to you shepherd," said one in a high and excited voice.

Another chimed in with an observation. "We have seen another human in the forest this morning. He seemed very nice, but I've never seen him before."

It's not unusual for the goat community to see angels; it's almost a daily occurrence. But a report like this from the squirrels was indeed peculiar.

"It could be an angel, my furry friend. You've seen them before," said Roee.

"No, no, no, no, no," said Nuttrum. "This one was happy. I have never seen an angel laugh."

After a few minutes of squirrel talk, Roee thanked them for taking time from their busy schedule, blessed them and tucked the information away for processing. He excused himself and continued his hike to the Rock.

The last ten minutes to Vision Rock is a semi-steep and exhilarating climb. The shepherd loved this part because it left him limber and breathing hard. As he stood catching his breath at the top, he looked out over Wonder Valley, the vistas beyond the surrounding mountains and marveled with gratefulness at the privilege he'd been given to live here.

Removing his backpack with its bottles of water, he made the connective thought to what he felt about the forest atmosphere. "It's friendlier than normal today," he thought out loud.

"Yeah, that's the same thing I was thinking," came a voice from behind.

Hearing another voice didn't surprise Roee; the squirrel report prepared him for that. But when he turned around, he saw a familiar face. A man wearing camouflage, a hunting bow with a quiver of arrows and one of the biggest and most loving smiles he had seen since the last time they were together in the camp.

"Good morning my friend," said the man.

The Hunter

"Good morning Jesus. What a beautiful surprise," responded Roee warmly.

Jesus grabbed him by the shoulders, looked into his eyes then wrapped him in a bear hug. As they released, Jesus gave the shepherd a knuckle rub on his forehead.

"I've been looking forward to some quality time with you Roee. This is going to be the high point of my day. I actually get a chance to tell you how much I love you face to face."

Jesus did a fist pump, looked at Roee and said, "This is exciting!" And with that he enthusiastically hugged him again.

Roee and Jesus started laughing for the happiness of being together.

"This is amazing," said Roee. "I wasn't expecting to see you."

"I love surprises as much as you love my mysteries. It's fun to watch your reaction. You handled it like its normal. You didn't freak out at all. What's with that?"

"It was the squirrels. They ratted on ya."

"I knew it! I love those guys, but I should have said something."

"I don't think they should have to keep secrets, Jesus. They're natural chatter boxes. They'd explode trying to keep it in"

"You're right about that."

"So, wow! This is a first. You came here so you could spend some casual time with me?"

"That's right. I've always wanted to do that. And we have sort of done it many times in the past. But today I wanted to bless you with something special. Papa told me you could ask any question you wanted to."

"Really? Anything?"

"Yeah, ask whatever you want, but it has to be something fun. Ask me something fun."

"This is quite a unique opportunity. But nothing serious?"

"That's right. Orders from the Holy Ghost!"

"Of all the theological and spiritual questions I have bouncing around in my skull, I can't ask a serious question?.....This is a hoot. I'm tempted to scream "unfair."

"I know, Roee," said Jesus using full arm language to make emphasis. "A once in a lifetime experience wasted on fun. The injustice of it is simply dastardly."

Jesus and Roee had a good laugh at not only the human thinking behind the statement, but also the out-of-the-box incongruence of the moment.

On the outside Roee laughed because of his love for the one who stood before him. But inside was a chafing on his human reason. And he knew that Jesus knew what he was feeling, which caused him to laugh at himself.

"Give me a moment, Jesus. My humanity needs to quiet itself. And I know you know why. And thanks for your patience. You know that I love you."

"I know what you're feeling. And I'll give you a minute to let your heart catch up with my purposes. Papa knew you wouldn't like it at first. But trust me, the memory of this moment will last a lot longer than any serious knowledge I could give you."

"I can see that, Jesus. It's like a father and son outing. We're just enjoying the time together."

"Yup, that's how I feel about it. So what do you have?"

Roee mulled over the myriad serious questions he had always wanted to explore. Then some that had more ethereal implications. Then, landed on one that he felt would be amusing.

"Is there life on other planets in this universe of ours?"

"I like that question. That's a good one Roee."

"I will tell you about the universe first, then I will tell you about life....out there."

When he said "out there," he laughingly drew out the phrase with long and loud embellishment; his arms spread to outer space.

"As you already know, Lucifer was with us in what you call heaven. Heaven is actually a place inside another place. But that idea will be explored later. So let's just say for the sake of discussion that at that time, there was no other place than heaven. It's a place made up entirely of our presence and our living creation. Our presence; that is the presence of Papa, Holy Spirit and myself; illuminates everything. There is no need for stars, suns or moons. There was no such place that contained darkness at that time that needed to be lit up."

"When Lucifer was judged for his plot to divide the inhabitants of our creation and make himself their god we had to create a place for him and all those that believed his lies that was outside our presence. And so, without our presence there is no light."

"So we fashioned an area outside heaven that had no substance, life or order where they could be taken. Until that point, all of creation was unaware of anything called darkness."

"It was then that Lucifer was cast down in a simple gesture like lightning along with those who chose to follow him. I was a witness to that event as you know. It was a sad day for me to see so many old friends I did life with leave my Father's presence. But Papa was adamant."

"He didn't want his loved ones to be with him if they were going to continue in rebellion against him. He patiently corrected and admonished them until they chose the point of no return. They no longer had the ability to turn back and face Daddy and his Lordship. Once that line was crossed, there was no other wisdom that could redeem the situation. His Kingdom was divided and it could not remain that way."

"So we and our choir gang sang this universe and this planet into existence. It was a bitter sweet time for us. It was sad that it had to be done at all. But it also started a mystery amongst us because we know the heart of Papa."

"But getting back to creation, we created a place where our presence was totally absent and put Lucifer and his followers there."

Roee jumped in with another question.

"That seems like a lot of extra darkness if he is only confined to earth isn't it?"

Jesus laughed. "Yeah, in a human thinking kind of way it is. But what's a few thousand light years of real estate to someone who can create as much as he wants?"

"Since you put it that way Jesus, I know it's beyond me to comprehend. But maybe you could give it a try. Why all the darkness? And if I understand the scientists correctly, why is it still growing?"

"Okay, here's the over-simplification of it. If you were to take a golf ball and stick it in the middle of an eighteen hole golf course, build a housing development around that, you would have how big this golf ball universe is compared to our presence in heaven."

"But life is not static, it continues to expand and multiply; including dark life. Stars and planets are formed with the expansion of darkness. Light and darkness will continue to expand together until the time when darkness will be judged and eliminated."

"As with all metaphor, that explanation doesn't do it justice. But I think you get the idea."

"In an overwhelming sort of way, yeah. I think I get it. But still, there's no real way for man to figure it out. Seems like overkill to me. There's a lot of marvel and beauty out there we as humankind will probably never see nor understand why it's there."

"If it helps any Roee, we like to have fun too. Creativity gets in your blood. None of the heavenly artists I know care if someone else sees their handiwork. But it's there to look at if someone wanted to look at it. You'd be astonished at the magnificent creative designs that are inside what you call a black hole. Some of the guys have created the wildest masterpieces there."

"Wow, I can't wait to see them."

"Unfortunately, they won't be there when this is all over. I'll have to figure out a way to make pictures of them for you. But I don't think you'll be very impressed once you see heaven. What the guys have done out there is like what graffiti artists have done to beautify ghettos."

Roee laughed at the comparison then said, "Okay, I think I'm getting it. Compared to heaven, all this is pretty ugly."

"Without our direct life and light from our presence, what else could it be? You've seen the stuff they take pictures of through telescopes. Nothing looks good up close. And that's where art is appreciated the most; up close for the hidden meanings and mysteries."

The Hunter

"Okay. Well speaking of life, is there anything out there?"

"Nothing human. Nothing that you can see. It doesn't matter how big a telescope is built or how far out you put it. Man will not find what he's looking for. In the mean time, a lot of my greatest artists are out there having fun making stuff.....Sure messes with the mystique, doesn't it?"

"That's an understatement. You said this universe thing will all be gone? What's with that?

"I've been talking about it since Isaiah 65; or at least since the days of Isaiah. Peter caught a glimpse of it and John had a revelation about it. All of what you see will eventually be dissolved in fire. This earth will be gone. Darkness will be gone. And if you can picture it, this universe will be gone in the wildest display of flames you've ever seen. And as Isaiah said, when it's all over, no one will even remember it."

"In the process of demolition of the old, we will create some new stuff. The new Jerusalem is already built. It's just waiting for the right moment to be revealed. Trust me, you'll love it."

"You had a glimpse of things not too long ago when I brought my goat buddies up for a visit. Did you want to come back to this?"

"No....but yes. But it wasn't because of the view or aesthetics."

"I know. And I love you for it. You were good about

coming back because you love like I do. That was huge Roee. Thanks. Even though you didn't have a say in the issue, you didn't resist or complain. There's been a ton of people who had to come back that didn't want to because their work wasn't finished."

"Speaking of goats," said Roee, "that reminds me of a fun question I have about them."

"Are the new babies going to be talkers too? Are we going to replenish the earth with this new breed of goats?"

"That's two questions, and the answers are yes, and sort of. All the new generations will talk and build on the giftings I've given this one. But they're not going to fill the earth like people do. There's not enough time left in the age for that. When the final harvest is complete, I'll fulfill my promise to them and bring them home."

"They represent an unusual sign and wonder. And I'm sure it has you wondering, doesn't it?"

"I'm wondering if you could elaborate on what you're going to do with them."

"Not now. But you'll know and see soon enough. It'll be fun. Trust me, I know you'll like it."

The first rays of light were peaking over the crowns of the distant mountains like a little boy peering cautiously over a fence. Discovering the coast to be clear, he decided he could go over the top boldly.

Jesus and Roee simultaneously began to sing a

The Hunter

song in praise of Papa's goodness and sat cross-legged on the rock to enjoy the moment. The two shepherds were caught up in gratitude for these sweet moments of intimacy together.

With the passing of several minutes, Jesus picked two leaves from a plant that had grown in a crack in the rock and handed one to Roee. Jesus popped one in his mouth and motioned for Roee to do the same.

"It's mint! That wasn't there before! Dodee would love this for her tea. I suppose it's a dumb question, but how did you do that?"

Jesus laughed......"It's a gift I have."

"There's a fresh batch of wild bergamot around here too. I know you like it with your tea. I'll show you where to find it later."

"Son, have you given any more thought to starting a garden? You guys could use the fresh food."

"It's pretty late in the season to start new seedlings. But you know that don't you. Why do you ask?"

"Considering all the creative power Holy Spirit has put in this valley, natural cycles as you know them aren't a big part of the equation any more. Whatever seeds you have will produce super foods quickly. You've been preaching about a new normal. Have some fun and explore the possibilities I've put here. The results will surprise you."

Jesus put his fist out and Roee held out his hands

to receive. He rained a dozen or so seeds into them.

"These are brand new. They've never been grown before," Jesus said with a smile.

"Plant them about ten feet apart and let them run wild. They're yummy and nutritious. It's a squash variety that gets large enough for a meal and will keep well into winter and early spring. At the end of their growing season, the goats will enjoy the green plants you pull up and you can start something else in their place. It's the crop rotation thing to do."

"Keep all the seeds. You can save a couple dozen for the next planting, then package and trade the rest for other seeds from the local guys. In a year, you could have quite a farm."

"Thank you. Maybe I can call them wonder squash."

Jesus laughed and said, "How about a name with some chutzpah. Taste it first before you name it. Show me your creativity."

"Again, thanks. It's exciting to grow new stuff. It's like a new mystery to solve. What will the outcome be?"

"Yup......the angels and saints in heaven have that same excitement about what's happening in this valley."

Some moments of quietness gave Roee the opportunity to explore his imagination for another fun question. The funny thing is, the left half of his brain was screaming for deeper questions to be put forth. But Roee kept telling it that this was his right brained time for relaxed and fun creativity. Something might be in it for lefty in the leftovers.

"I have another question."

"Fire away."

"What's the story on dinosaurs?"

"Ahhhh.....you may find that answer a little disappointing because it's so simple. Daddy once quipped: 'Yesterdays dinosaur is tomorrows fuels.'"

"Coal, natural gas and petroleum to name a few is a byproduct of that era. And diamonds are a byproduct of the other. Those large animals left a lot of organic matter in the ground while they were here. It's proof that Papa was planning ahead for the needs of the modern age."

"Very creative, but not necessarily the big story all the archeologists make it out to be. Like the universe and man's fascination with what's out there, man is also obsessed with what once was and builds legends and opinions to make an interesting accounting for it. The evolution lie got started for a lack of perspective about that age."

"It was during Papa's opening moves of his plan of creation and redemption. The actual story involves the realm of eternity and what Papa was doing with Lucifer then. For now that part of the story doesn't need to be told because Lucifer's destiny has been judged, yet he remains an adversary. It's complicated and he would twist the story to distract from man's need for a redeemer."

"He's not the victim. Man is his victim and I came to deliver all men from his power and bring them into relationship with Papa."

"What do you mean about their lack of perspective about that age?"

"Allow me to answer your question with a question."

"On what day was time created?"

"That's easy," Roee boldly proclaimed with a gleam in his eye. "It was Wednesday."

"I love it," chuckled Jesus and slapping his knee. "That's funny."

"Okay, it was the fourth day."

"You have a marvelous imagination. Use it for a minute to run through the first three days in wild abandon; no restraints. What could you picture if the creation of light in the darkness, the development of atmospheres, the separation of land and water and the beginning of all vegetation was all done in three distinct days without the existence of time?"

"Without any thought at all, the first thing is that the definition of a day would take on new meaning. And I don't feel like I have the capacity to grasp it like I can grasp real time. I've tried that before. The more I run with it, I think I need another something-or-other to truly get it. It would drive myself crazy trying to see it."

"Is that eternity?"

"It's eternity without God; chaos and emptiness heading in a brand new direction of order and fulfillment. But much happened to bring God into those first eternal days that is beyond the mind of man to comprehend. And what Papa reveals about those days is only as deep as man is able to understand; which isn't much in his current form."

"So what form does he need?'

"I will show you in a minute. But first he needs to know that his primary objective is not to understand creation. He is designed to intimately know his creator."

"And now I will show you what that looks like. Let's stand together facing each other and I'll show you what form man needs."

In that position, Jesus quickly turned from human to brilliant light and entered the body of Roee.

From somewhere inside, Jesus said, "Can you hear me now?"

Roee started laughing and said, "That tickles.....just kidding. Yeah, I hear you."

"Listen to this, 'Christ in you the hope of glory.'"

"And this: 'Father, may they be one as we are one.'"

"To the natural man it's a mystery. To the spiritual man, it's a necessity; it's the most important thing you will want to treasure. Because all that other stuff wasn't around, nor will be, when you arrive at your destination."

"Any other questions?"

"Give me a few minutes.....but while you're there," Roee said jokingly, "feel free to make yourself at home. There's a couple cold root beers in the fridge."

From somewhere within he heard laughter and the sound of a bottle cap popping.

The Hunter

TRANSITION

Perhaps Papa gives us seasons to help us realize the idea
that change should be an element of our thinking. For
some people that may not be as active a reality as it is
with others. And the differences are more acute for those
who like things to remain the same.

The short days of winter give minds and bodies
natural rest and a time to contemplate what's ahead.
The beauty of spring stimulates the soul with color
and warmth as the plans calculated during the winter
are now ready to bloom into production. Fall draws us
gradually away as we wind down from the long days and
hard work of a productive summer. Once done we can
count our blessings with gratefulness.

In Wonder Valley the summer months had been
busy building days.

Roee and Shamus built the fireplace and chimney
for the cabin spending cool morning hours building
layers of rock with mortar. The heat of the afternoon air
cured their progress while they focused on other things.
Using scrap pieces of plywood and building progressively,
they managed an arched fireplace. With it complete and
cured, the remainder of the chimney and mantle stacked
up perfectly.

Rigo and Jacob showed up in late June with a load

of roofing shingles. Being a small cabin, four hard workers had it complete and rainproof in half a day. The summer thunder storms tested their expertise with a passing grade.

After Roee's visit with Jesus, he, Dodee and Shamus went to work on a garden in earnest near the creek where water could be pumped readily. Shamus made a trip to Little Faith in his Jeep to borrow a rototiller, additional gasoline and as much chain-link fencing as he could carry.

It's laughable to think a wilderness garden would need a fence around it. But anyone who knows deer and goats knows the wisdom of it. In the end, Shamus required a second outing for more fencing and sturdier posts.

On the second trip, Roee went along. A stop at Shamus' old digs allowed them to pick up whatever personal items he wanted to keep. Reflecting on the New Testament example of Zacchaeus he felt that any cash and bank accounts he had could be assets for current purchases and future needs.

While there he gave away belongings that no longer held personal value to the girls who worked for him. He also released them from further obligation to him and they were free to go.

Roee and Shamus spent the better part of several hours talking with the girls about what Jesus had done to bring changes to Shamus' life. The difference in him was undeniable. He was no longer the man the girls remembered.

The two prayed for the girls' future and welfare and their physical ailments; seeing remarkable results. The encounter turned into an awakening of spiritual hunger in all but the most wounded girls. In wrapping up, the guys encouraged them to connect with Rigo, Jacob and the gang to get them going in a positive spiritual direction.

The outing ignited a fire in Shamus. He wanted to help get these girls, and girls like them, away from the clutches of this hideous lifestyle. Having been away for awhile, its darkness and its impact on humanity shook his insides.

As the duo drove away that day in early July, a weight of urgency bore down on therm both. But Roee knew that without a collective unity in the believing neighborhood, any success would be short lived. Papa had a plan. It was obvious in all that had transpired since the shepherds had come to the valley.

"Roee, if we can't figure out a way to get these girls off the streets, the other pimps will move in and take over their lives; they're just too vulnerable."

"You saw the looks on their faces, they want what we have. What can we do?"

'Shamus, let's drop by Jacob and Anna's store and see if we can pull a meeting together with the gang. We need ideas and we need to know what kind of resources we have. We may need to spend the night before we head back. So let's just settle in until we see movement."

A few calls by Jacob and a meeting came together for the evening. Rigo and Maria cancelled an appointment they had, but everybody else was available. The meeting was scheduled for sevenish at Jacob and Anna's.

With snacks and drinks laid out, the team trickled in over a forty-five minute span. Discussion started in a serious vein about seven forty-five.

Shamus and Roee mapped out the events of the day with the girls in Lawless and the concerns those events raised about having a place where trafficking people could escape the magnetic tentacles of their former life.

Good ideas flowed well about having a home built on one or two of the farms there in Little Faith where people could learn the agricultural life. They also discussed the potential for those places to be halfway or reentry places but not necessarily a sanctuary for an exit from the industry. Something in Wonder Valley would be ideal for that purpose. Its remoteness lent to a natural security buffer.

Rigo and Maria had an unused satellite phone from when they lived in rural Texas that could help with communications. The minutes were expensive but could be a practicality if used frugally. Incoming texts were typically free. Keeping it charged could be accomplished with Shamus' Jeep until a generator or solar panel was installed.

When the subject shifted to housing, the prospect

Transition

of needing serious money changed the focus. Another small log home would not be practical given the size of facility needed for three or four girls. And with sanitation being a current minor issue, it would become a major one with the additional people.

Del volunteered to look into modular building possibilities and see where it would take him. Rigo took on the assignment of self-composting sanitation or even a septic system for the amount of people they were discussing.

And Jacob would call Burnus to see what packages were available for the satellite phone. When approved by the group he would make a trip there to activate it.

The ladies enthusiastically set their hearts to networking among the neighbors and churches for potential fundraising. The ideas were typical for bake sales and extended friends and family to make contributions. It was a worthy cause and the general feeling was confidence in the community pulling together.

As creativity grew beyond the obvious, plans of a self-sustaining industry to pour funds into their ideas became part of the equation. The vision of the group was forming clearer and shaping into a doable adventure.

Roee raised a concern that had been niggling at his mind.

"As it stands, our valley is virtually untouched by the outside world. If we are to protect the security of these ladies, we need to keep our location private until further notice; on a need to know basis. Perhaps we could make Little Faith a base and use it to screen who goes in and out."

"Can I get your cooperation on that?"

The team saw the wisdom in his thinking.

Rigo scored a breakthrough two weeks after the meeting. A local septic service donated the basic materials for a five thousand gallon septic tank plus the parts for a large leach field.

With all the farms, borrowing a backhoe was a simple task. Every busy farm had at least one. The strategic difficulty of getting it into Wonder Valley simply revolved around the time it would take to get it there and back.

The septic service offered the use of their truck to get the tank and other supplies delivered when they had a lull in business. That opportunity arrived in a last minute call toward the end of July. Within a week of that call, the system was installed and the backhoe returned.

Other ideas included a bath house and drilling a well for water supply.

Somewhere during the septic project, the satellite phone was activated with a minimum of minutes to use. If more minutes were needed, it could be determined later.

Even with the addition of a few modern conveniences, the rustic feel of the valley hadn't changed significantly. It was foreseen that when the digging area from the septic system regained its green growth, the changes wouldn't be noticed.

Word got around about the project, and a used portable bath house was donated by the local forestry department. It had been used by them a few times for a firefighting base camp. Getting it there through the rough trail and terrain took a gentle and patient touch. It was a welcomed accomplishment.

Once there, it was conveniently parked and leveled for use. With all the plumbing hooked up, an old fashioned water wheel built at the stream provided a crude but effective means to get water to it until something better could be arranged. The pressure wasn't much, but it functioned. Even without the comfort of hot water, Dodee was happy.

The topic of building a house in the valley came up again at a meeting about a month after the first one. Del's thorough research produced a practical game plan for putting together something simple. In the process, he had shown himself to be a strong administrator and was officially given those reigns.

"What I found for the situation we have in the valley, is practical and buildable with the manpower and skills we have available. It is called a "panelized home kit" and can be put together in bundles small enough to trailer into the valley without having to cut down any trees along the way. It would take careful site planning and foundation work to prepare the way in advance. But once started, they tell me the basic shell can theoretically be complete in a week or so. With a lot of blessing, the inside can be finished over the winter months and open for people by spring. That, of course depends on when we get started."

"So what does the cost look like, Del?" asked Roee.

"For a simple design, about fifty-five dollars a square foot."

"Then size kind of depends on how much money we can raise," said Roee. "Any idea on projections?"

"It's still too early to tell, Roee. But the interest is gaining some momentum. With prayer, anything is possible."

"Gosh Del," wondered Maria, "with some design planning, maybe we could include a little shop space for mohair production. We could sell it from here and help sustain other needs in a small way."

"I like that idea," said Dodee.

"I guess," said Del, "the next phase of things is to set a target for how much we need to get started and go public with fundraising."

"That area's not my bailiwick," responded Shamus. "With all the stone we have up there, why don't we build us an Irish castle instead?"

"Aye, that sounds like a keen thing to do, Shamus," said Roee in some kind of mock-Celtic accent. "But have ye checked recently to see how loong it takes to build the likes of a wee castle? And finding a master castle builder these days," he said with a slight twitch of his head. "I dunno."

"Maybe we can put that into our long range planning. It would so fit in with the landscape, Roee."

"Seriously guys," injected Del. "We should have somebody, somewhere in the community who knows how to fundraise well without getting people offended. It has the potential for being a sensitive subject. But it has very strong possibilities for getting us started."

"Okay," said Roee. "Let's tag that as the next step forward."

"I have another concern that I'd like to bring up. It may or may not be a big deal. But I think it would be wisdom to know something about it now that we are noticeably developing up there."

"Is there any way we can find out who owns the property in Wonder Valley?"

That notion caught every mind off guard and there was brief silence.

"Wow Roee, I'm a good snoop dog," inserted Jacob. "I like doing that kind of stuff, I got a nose for it. I'll look into it."

"I have something I'd like to talk with Maria about before we move on to anything else," stated Dodee.

"What's that, Dodee," asked Maria.

"I don't know a thing about mohair and when to do sheering and all that. When's a good time to do sheering and how do we groom the gang up there for good quality?"

"I can come up with a generator and some electric sheers when the time is right; which should be soon. They should be sheered twice a year. At that time I can teach you some basics about it."

"The first batch of hair may need to be discarded or burned. It won't have any commercial value. But maybe it can be used for something as a filler. We'll talk more about it later. We don't want to bore these gringos with that stuff."

"Thanks Maria. I'll look forward to having a few days with you. We can have some girl time."

"Maybe Anna and I can come with you Maria," said Kathy. "We haven't been up there yet and we are dying to see the place and learn how to talk goat with the best of 'em."

"I love that idea, Kathy" said Anna. "We can let the guys man the fort for a few days and we gals can have a little retreat."

"Alrighty then," said Del with a chuckle. "Looks like you gals just need to fix a date for that."

"Now that you mountain folk are in the twenty-first century with a phone and all, we'll text you when we know something."

"Anything else on your minds?" continued Del.

"Okay. I declare all serious talk over with. Let's have some fun."

"Speaking of fun," responded Dodee with a knowing look on her face."I have a fun announcement to make. Roee and I are with child. And as best I can figure, we will be due sometime in early spring."

Even as she was making the announcement, congratulations, praise and yippees flew in all directions. With the excitement level ramping up a couple notches, snacks and drinks were broken out to celebrate.

Dodee looked compassionately into Maria's eyes for signs of sadness. But Maria's face was soft with the tender tears of joy.

"I love you dearly, my friend," said Maria. "How could I not be happy for you and only sad for me. My day will come. But this is your day and I see in your face a promise for my future. I feel only a full and happy heart and a joyful awareness of my Jesus' presence."

Their embrace was long and filled with laughter.

During this season, the herd wasn't doing any great adventures. But honestly, they liked that. For now, their routine consisted of memorizing the gospels and enjoying a spiritual lifestyle that many Christians were unaware of. Being accustomed to a peaceable life, the goats found that alone as being exciting.

They had come from being ordinary goats to being extraordinary goats; super goats if you ask Willie. Their normal was so far out of any box, you'd think they were crackers. But, that was their new reality. And they were simply getting used to it. In the course of time, another normal would come that would radically pale to the one they had been given.

For now, they were in training and learning to be a team.

Jacob did his snooping around and found the owners of the property. The group was a holding company for investing in developments. Their plans for the valley was to create a resort area in time. But the current utilities development would be so costly they simply chose to leave the property for another generation to develop when public funds afforded getting electricity closer for their purposes.

Jacob and Rigo travelled for a face-to-face meeting and convinced them to come and see what was going on.

Their arrival was a testimony to Papa's foreknowledge about the hearts of men. They were captivated by what they saw and the plans they heard.....like those who had come to help build the cabin....they threw their involvement in with Papa's design and went home different people.

ON THE MOUNTAIN

A solitary figure sat on the rock shelf in high mountain terrain patiently watchful below him for a potential meal to make itself visible. In the waiting, he panned the skyline of distant peaks. On the taller crests were white caps of snow from an earlier fall storm. This was Nara's home and it was all that he had lived with.

His world was typically a realm of isolation and wilderness. He once had a mate. But she was killed by a rancher in the lower elevations before the cubs in her body were born. Strangely, he felt little grief over the loss but recognized that the atmosphere had been different when she was around. There had been someone to share life and thoughts and ideas with for at least the short while she was with him.

Over time he withdrew increasingly deeper into himself and became the only world he cared about. Communication with others focused on the design to control and manipulate for his advantage. Isolation increased. Other voices appeared convincing him they were his own. They sounded like him, but it wasn't his true heart. As the voices persisted, he could no longer differentiate which voice was his own from those that sucked him into increasing darkness.

Motives shifted along the way and he no longer killed just for food. Killing became a game of cruelty.

After awhile, even that wasn't diabolical enough. He stole lives from the wild goat herd for the sick satisfaction of making their lives miserably oppressive. A twisted scheme of crushing them into wretched creatures burned smiles across his face.

Ironically, the process of his slide into this dark realm created the fiendish makeover he now was. He too had become an unhappy and wretched creature.

Looking around at the magnificent landscape, the thought crept into his mind about how long it had been since he had peacefully enjoyed its beauty. He growled angrily at the inner critters that had been dominating him for so long. What had started as subtle companion voices were now an unwanted presence that gave him no rest. His sanctum had become an ugly and lonesome prison.

While processing these thoughts a landslide of rocks broke free somewhere behind him. Turning, he crouched quickly to see what it could be and readied to spring if it was a meal. He was hungry. There sat a hunter wearing camouflage fatigues and a bow draped across his left shoulder. A quiver half full of arrows was slung across his right shoulder. He sat with his knees up, his arms wrapped around his knees and his ankles crossed. His countenance revealed that he was unconcerned of any danger to himself.

Although unafraid, he had seen the work of hunters. Running was his only option. And the voices were shrieking hateful messages.

But this hunter was looking deep into Nara's eyes. "No," thought Nara, "he's looking into my soul." It unnerved him that someone could have access inside and find every hidden part of him. Every evil thought, all the past things he had done that no one but him knew about, and even the presence of the voices within him.

And yet, those eyes were filled with something he had only seen glimpses of in the valley. Nara recognized him. He had seen him around those crazy goats. He had been with the shepherd.

"I can get rid of those things for you if you want to be free," the man said.

"You're the shepherd's friend," said Nara rather uneasily. But he relaxed his crouch and took up a sitting position. He could still react swiftly if any aggression started.

"He's much more than a friend, Nara. He's a son and that means a lot to me."

To Nara, he was speaking a foreign language. The sentiments had no familiarity whatsoever.

"This thing inside me doesn't like you. It wants me to kill you."

"So why don't you?" asked Jesus without flinching. He was cancelling out Nara's options.

"It's a waste of time." Nara said sarcastically. It was his demons speaking. "I've seen what you do with the death I've created. You have some kind of magic powers."

"I have nothing but life within me, Nara. It has nothing to do with magic. I rule over death and demons. In time, everything will bow before me."

When Jesus said that, the creatures inside Nara trembled.

"I've never felt this before," Nara confessed. "What is this?"

"It's fear Nara."

"I've never known fear."

"And you've never known peace and love before either. If you want peace and love instead of fear and brutality, those things will have to leave. And they won't leave until you want them to."

Nara sat trembling and thinking for what seemed like several minutes as he stared out over the mountainous horizon. He turned to Jesus and said loudly, "I want to be free of this stuff!"

Jesus stood. "Leave him," Jesus said quietly and calmly.

Immediately Nara screamed then choked up two twin hairballs with large grotesque lips that covered the major portion of their bodies. The hairballs wriggled then squirmed like snakes over to the edge of the rock shelf in the opposite direction of Jesus then disappeared.

"That's it?" said Nara in disbelief. "That's all they are? They're nothing!"

"When you don't know the truth, they seem bigger than they really are. They're good liars and can be quite convincing. Haven't you used that strategy yourself on the ignorant and unsuspecting? Haven't you played on misguided dreams to destroy lives?"

"Yes, I suppose I have," Nara responded in shock. "But, I didn't know I was being duped by my own strategy! How stupid of me!"

"The striking difference between you and them is that you can act quite fierce and intimidating at times or appear to be a harmless cub. But your days of deception are over. They have been at it for quite a long time and will undoubtedly find another victim. Now that they're gone, you need something new."

And with that statement Jesus walked up and touched Nara, causing him to shriek. He sprinted off the rock shelf back into the dirt and down into the tree line like a playful kitten out of control. He could be heard yelling and laughing as he jumped into trees and down again, over rocks and a natural earth berm. He ran and roared and laughed for what appeared to be an hour then came charging back to Jesus. Jesus had been laughing as he approached and watched as Nara launched for a long pounce. He landed on Jesus knocking him to the ground. They wrestled and laughed playfully until Nara was exhausted, then both lay still while Nara panted heavily.

"Wow! What was that?"

"I haven't felt like that since I was a cub."

"That was my Spirit coming into and on you. It will

make you a new creature."

"I'm not going to be a lion anymore?"

Jesus laughed. "Nothing like that. You will always be a lion. But you can be a different type of lion now; a lion that can lay down with a lamb in peace. You can be a lion that can be a friend of mine instead of my enemy.......a lion that can love and have my power to demonstrate how much I love."

"I don't think I know much about love."

"I will show you, Nara."

"Will I still eat?"

"Yup," Jesus said with a smile. "Some things aren't going to change; at least not for awhile anyway."

"That could make for some unhappy goats."

"Ahhh, those who belong to me are not yours to eat. This is how you will know the difference; I have written the name of life on those who are mine. You will be able to see it from this day forward. And that will include people."

Jesus laughed then said, "But you're not allowed to kill and eat people."

"And now for the bad news," said Jesus with a broad smile.

Nara looked at him quizzically; not knowing what he meant by "bad news."

"There will be those who won't like you and don't want you around. But it is in the midst of that that I will teach you the ways of love. And you will learn to stand and be a mighty warrior for me because of it."

Nara looked at him strangely while wondering what he had gotten himself into. "Not being liked is nothing new. But I'd like to hang out with your goat friends and enjoy some peace and quiet for a change. Maybe I could make amends for all the harm I caused them."

"You can and you will," added Jesus. "We will be on our way to talk with them shortly for that very reason. But, it isn't going to be easy for some of them to forgive you."

"Yeah, I can see why."

"Besides that, you wouldn't like the easy and pastoral life they live. You would grow restless and bored. What I have in mind for you is suited just for you. And you're the only you in these woods. The most important person you will need to know is not the goats; it's me. You and I are going to spend a lot of time together while you learn what makes me tick and how to say the things I want said and the way I want things revealed to others. Spending that much time with me is not easy. Many have quit and settled for lesser callings because of its requirements."

"But I am confident that I have done well in choosing you, Nara."

"You chose me?" said Nara with a start. "When?"

"Before the beginnings of this creation I knew you would be here in this time and this space. I have been preparing you for my purposes even while you were wreaking havoc on those that I love."

It was a weighty revelation and caused Nara to consider all that he had done and where he had allowed himself to be taken in darkness. His mind spun in wonder.

"You were unaware of my presence and ignorant of my work in your life, of course. And that is why I can forgive all your wrong doing and remove even the history of it from my memory. The old Nara is dead if you will believe in me and accept the new life I am offering you."

Nara had been sitting and rose and lowered his head in respect and honor.

"I am undeserving and unworthy of your kindness my Lord. I make myself your slave and commit my life to your desire."

"Thank you, Nara, and that is a good starting place. But until you become my faithful companion you will not be ready for the work I have called you to do. You will learn how I feel and how I think. You will learn my ways and know my heart. I will train you to depend on me and my presence."

"I can see," began Nara soberly, "why you say it will be hard. I've never depended on anyone but myself all these years; except for those two idiot hairballs. I don't think I fully understand, but I am willing."

"I am patient and kind Nara. I have all confidence that I can create in you everything you will need to be my friend. It's up to you as to how long it will take."

"Why is that?" asked Nara.

"You have lived a long time serving your own desires and the desires of those two creatures that possessed you. Serving me well will come from a place of affection and commitment to my desires."

Nara sat down again and considered what was being asked and offered for a few minutes while Jesus gave him quiet space to consider his heart.

"I have only one more question."

Jesus looked at him kindly and humorously; knowing the question before Nara asked.

"Do I have to look ridiculously foolish like those goats do? All that prancing and stuff, I don't know if I can do that."

Jesus laughed openly while Nara chuckled mildly.

"In time, Nara, you will lose some of your refined sophistication. No, I give you the freedom to be yourself because I am just crazy in love with who you are."

"And now.....it is time for us to go visit our goat buddies. It's a long walk from here and I can use the time to teach you some basics."

Nara gracefully bounded off the rock ledge and headed down the mountain.

He stopped suddenly, turned and asked: "What is your name?"

To be continued....

On The Mountain

Author's Thoughts

Our generous God freely gives us every good and perfect gift. These wonderful gifts come down to us from the Father of lights, the unchanging God who shines from the heavens with no hidden shadow or hint of darkness." (James 1:17, The Passion translation)

The seed idea for the Renascence Series arrived Christmas day of 2014. It came as a thought that could have been overlooked or not taken seriously. In time it would have been forgotten like debris floating downstream on a river. Fortunately, I was alert and looking upstream because I had been expecting a gift. I had asked Papa for a mystery Christmas present that was carefully thought about by him and uniquely suited for me. It didn't surprise me that it would come without fanfare. I believe he enjoys the fun of checking to see if I'm paying attention.

I saw its arrival as a plainly wrapped thought that had to be unpacked and acted on. After finishing the project I was working on at the time, I jumped in and discovered an unprecedented creative flow that is now into its third book. This first book has been more than two years in the making and deserves my gratitude to several people for its reality.

My wife, Ann, championed the idea from the beginning and helped bring this work to life. Being the spouse of a writer is often a life of sacrifice. Few people are aware of the mind and world of a writer who spends hours in another realm and those occasions when ideas come when it's not convenient to write them down. It can be disruptive and disconnecting. She has handled it like a champion, and I crown her a valued partner and editor. She is a woman of valor in that regard and deserves my abundant gratitude. It would not have happened without her insight, encouragement and support.

Dean Braxton gave his permission to glean from his life-after-death experience. His insights are woven into several places in the story line by way of Carrie. It's risky to put that kind of reality into fiction because it can be easily dismissed by minds focused on earthly things. Thanks for being willing to risk, Dean. You could not have known when you randomly handed me a memory stick filled with recordings and writings that some of it would find its way here.

Scott and Lynne's ranch is where Ann and I got our GHDs. Two years of goat herding as caretakers at their mountain property was an education unlike any other. We learned lessons in humility, commitment, hard work and shared the sorrows of losses to mountain lions and the elements and the joys of the many births of some of the cutest babies on the planet.

Wonder Valley has a resemblance to their ranch. Its essence inspired it. And their goats....oh yes. The names have been changed, but they are real. And they do talk; at least to me; in a language that can only be understood when the heart is open to hear them.

Thanks Scott and Lynne, Torsten, Isaiah and Elijah for being a part of the journey and your continuing friendship.

Thanks to Margaret Cantrell at Encouraging Word Publishing Services in Redding, CA for editing this book during a difficult personal season for her. It was an interesting journey as we built a friendship, and I'm looking forward to the next round.

Thank you Richard Nash for the final read through and writer's insights that you shared. And thanks for being a friend for forty years.

The drawings are courtesy of my niece, Donna Rey. Thanks for pulling the pictures from words off the page. That's not easy. I appreciate your creativity and readiness to take on the project.

And thank you Mickey and Kris Hatfield at Mama Too's Southern Seasoning for spicing this project forward. You believed without seeing. That's faith.